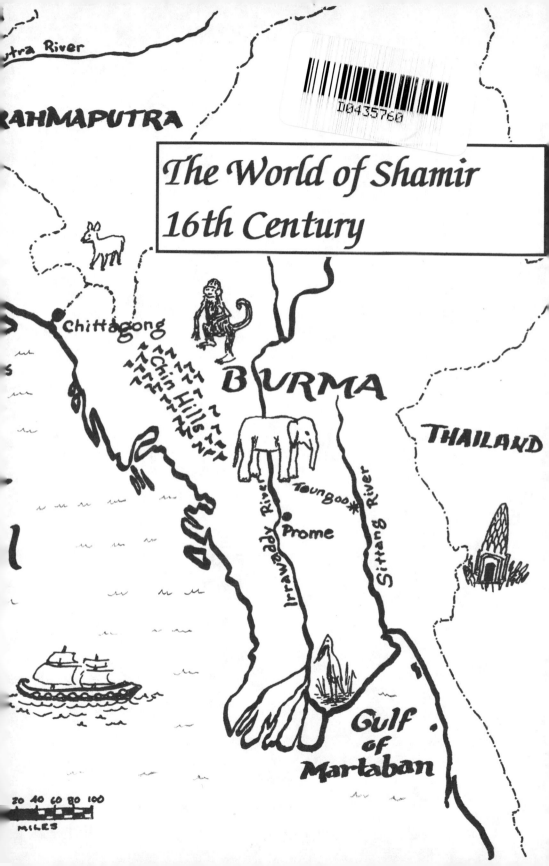

utra River

RAHMAPUTRA

D0435760

The World of Shamir 16th Century

Chittagong

Chin Hills

BURMA

THAILAND

Irrawaddy River

Toungoo

Prome

Sittang River

Gulf of Martaban

20 40 60 80 100
MILES

SHAMIR,
THE WHITE
ELEPHANT

A Rain Forest
Adventure

by
Beverly Croskery

Illustrated by
Bonny Bregante

Bell-Forsythe Publishing Company

First Edition 1997
Typesetting: Bell-Forsythe Publishing Company, Cincinnati, OH
Printed by C.J. Krehbiel Company, Cincinnati, OH

Publisher's Cataloging-in-Publication
(Provided by Quality Books, Inc.)

Croskery, Beverly F.
        Shamir, the white elephant : a rain forest adventure / by
    Beverly Croskery ; illustrated byBonny Bregante. -- 1st ed.
        p. cm
        Preassigned LCCN: 97-93252
        ISBN: O-9657619-4-0
        SUMMARY: A rare white elephant, born along the Ganges
    River, is befriended by an albino monkey, in this story set in
    16th century India.

        1. Elephants--India--Juvenile fiction. 2. Monkeys--India--
    Juvenile fiction.   3. India-- Juvenile fiction.   4. Mogul
    Empire--Juvenile fiction.   I. Bregante, Bonny. II. Title

    PZ10.3.C76Sha 1997   [Fic]
                                      QBI97-40558

SHAMIR, THE WHITE ELEPHANT

A Rain Forest Adventure

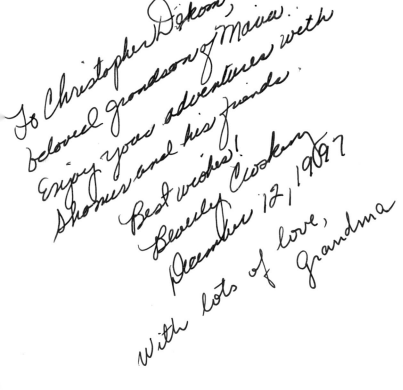

To Christopher Dickson,
beloved grandson of Mava.
Enjoy your adventures with
Shamir and his friends.
Best wishes!
Beverly Croskery
December 12, 1997
With lots of love,
Grandma

This book is dedicated to:

my husband, Robert;

my children
Richard, Robert, Kathryn and
Virginia;

my grandchildren
Robin, Thomas, Griffith,
Virginia, Caroline, and Nicole;

and to the students and staff at
Welch Elementary School.

You have all inspired me and made
Shamir live.

Introduction

This is a make-believe story about elephants. However, even though the characters are make believe, most of the facts about the living habits of elephants are true. Also, the geographical facts are as accurate as could be determined by the author.

The desire for white elephants and white monkeys during the sixteenth century is also true. Wars were fought and great lengths were taken to secure white elephants for the royal household. Small monkeys were also often captured and trained to entertain at court. White monkeys were also extremely rare and would be considered very valuable. While white elephants could survive quite well in the forest, albino monkeys would have difficulty in the wild.

At the time of this story, the country which is now Bangledesh was a part of the Mogul kingdom of India, ruled by Akbar. Much of the story takes place along the Ganges River in that area and in what is still India. Burma, where the rest of the story takes place, is now called Myanmar. In

1

the mid to late sixteenth century it was ruled by Burengnong. With the exception of Burengnong and Akbar, the names used in the story are fictional.

My family helped a great deal in bringing *Shamir* to fruition. In order to help readers understand the historical and geographical setting of *SHAMIR*, I asked my son, Richard, to create the map seen inside both the front and back covers of the book. My other son, Robert, took care of the many legal details in preparing the book for publication. Daughters, Virginia and Kathryn took time from their busy lives to read and critique the book, sometimes by way of FAX. My husband, Robert, encouraged me at every step of the way, proofreading and offering invaluable suggestions. Granddaughter, Robin, was the first sixth grader to read *Shamir*. She also offered good ideas. While other grandchildren could not yet read the book, Thomas, Griffith, Virginia and Caroline certainly enjoyed listening to the story, and Nicole offered encouragement.

Welch Elementary School, where I was once principal, invited me to share the story as a visiting author. For a week, we worked together through the first draft of the story. The staff and students were wonderful and several revisions were made as the result of their suggestions.

A special acknowledgement is made to Peter Jackson, author of ELEPHANTS, a part of the *Endangered Species* series, published by Chartwell Books. While I read many books, articles and reference materials to ensure accuracy, none were so helpful as the book by Peter Jackson. His insights gave me not only love and respect for elephants but a desire to help ensure that these gentle giants will remain a part of the wild kingdom forever.

Beverly Croskery

1

Shamir Finds a Friend

Once upon a time, many years ago, when the forests of India were thick and lush, and there was plenty of land for both elephants and people, huge herds of these magnificent beasts roamed the territory, feasting on the lush vegetation.

In a thick forested area along the Ganges River, there dwelt a large herd of elephants. In this herd there was born to Maru, daughter of Hannah, queen of the herd, an unusual yet beautiful elephant we shall call, Shamir. Shamir was a very special elephant. Elephants are usually gray, which is a good color for the forested area, and is to be expected. However, instead of gray, Shamir was white in color. Because a white elephant was extremely rare in the elephant kingdom, it was highly prized by kings and princes. In fact, wars had been fought over the number of white elephants in a king's stable.

Regardless of his color, Shamir's mother loved him very much. Maru also sensed that, because he was different, he would need extra care and would have to be closely watched.

Keeping a close watch on Shamir was not easy. He loved to explore. He took delight in walking through the forest and seeking out the extra tasty plants. He liked to slosh through the River Ganges and feel the cool water over his thick body. The muddy water was cool, and he especially liked to make mud packs and plaster them on top of his head. Such a wonderful feeling to have a cool mud pack on his head! Sometimes he emerged from the water looking, not white, but rather a muddy brown.

While Shamir, the baby elephant, had his happy moments, he was also sometimes very sad. Sometimes the thing which makes one rare and special, also makes one seem different to others. Even though his mother Maru would stroke him with her trunk gently and say, "Shamir, you are a beautiful and wonderful elephant,"

and even though his grandmother, the powerful and wise Hannah, who was the leader of the herd and most respected of all elephants would exclaim, "Ah Shamir, what a fine and beautiful, and clever elephant you are,"

still, Shamir was not happy, because he was very lonely.

There were several other young elephants in the herd. Shamir watched as they would join trunks and chase one another, trumpeting gleefully. But, when the other elephant young saw him coming to play, they would turn away from him. Many times, Shamir found himself looking at a circle of elephant tails. When this happened, he would sniffle quietly and slowly find his way to his mother, Maru.

"It will be all right, Shamir", promised Maru.

"They will play with you and be your friends, someday," assured his grandmother, Hannah.

Right now, this was small comfort to Shamir. He was all the more lonely as he watched the others romp together.

He did so long for a playmate! A huge tear could often be seen trickling over the white wrinkled cheek of little Shamir.

The elephant herd was often looking for a new home. Since even one elephant can eat a great deal of food in a short period of time, an entire herd can clear an area of the forest rather quickly.

Shamir stayed close to his mother, Maru, as the elephant herd moved through the forest seeking a new home. Hannah was always in the lead. She knew all the places to look for traps and she knew where the trees were fruiting and where there was plenty of water for bathing and drinking. No one ever moved out ahead of Hannah.

Once when they were moving through the forest, feasting on the lush vegetation, Hannah stopped in her tracks. All the other elephants did the same. She lifted her head high and motioned with her trunk for all to be quiet. There was the smell of fire in the air and the thundering sound made by many running elephants was heard. In the distance Hannah could see another herd of elephants on the run. They were surrounded by fire and were being driven by elephant catchers riding on the backs of trained elephants called "koonkies". Hannah knew they were witnessing the dreaded KHEDDA. This is the method used to capture an entire herd at one time. A fire surrounds the elephants except for one open area.

"Hasti! Hasti!" cried the catchers, as they drove the elephants along the carefully selected pathway.

The captured elephants trumpeted loudly, but obediently stayed inside the wall of fire created by the catchers. Hannah knew that the herd was being driven toward a place invisible to them, but known to her. It was a place called a stockade, where the elephants would be trapped and led away into captivity.

Without making a sound, Hannah turned in the opposite direction and the entire herd turned with her. She began to move silently and swiftly through the forest, followed by the herd. She stopped only long enough to sniff for signs of man and the pitfalls they may have lain. With catchers in the area, traps were expected. Many elephants have fallen into these pits which are huge holes dug by the catchers. They cover the pits with tree branches and other vegetation which will break easily with the weight of a elephant. Hannah did not want to lose any of her herd to these pits. The herd traveled day and night until they were many miles from the fire and could no longer hear or see the trapped elephants. They stopped to rest on the banks of the Ganges, far downstream of where they had been only a few hours before.

The next morning, Shamir awoke to the sound of singing birds, small animals scampering about the forest and monkeys swinging through the trees. Shamir decided to take a walk and look over his new surroundings.

He slipped unnoticed through the trees and into a small clearing. It was a beautiful day for a walk, and he was very hungry. As he was walking along, he suddenly heard strange scolding noises. He looked up to see two monkeys in the tree above him. One was hitting the other and seemed to be very angry. The monkey being beaten was holding his ears as if to shut out the noise and the hurt.

Shamir noted that this monkey was white! (He was what is called an albino monkey.)

Shamir immediately felt sorry for him and without hesitation, reached up and slapped the angry scolding monkey with his trunk, sending him reeling. The monkey scurried quickly away whimpering loudly as he swung through the trees.

"Thank you, my friend", said the white monkey.

"You are welcome", responded Shamir. "Why was he so angry with you?"

"I don't really know. I guess it is because I look different than the other monkeys. When I look at my reflection in the great Ganges River, I see a very ordinary looking monkey. The only difference is that I am white."

Suddenly he stopped and stared at Shamir.

"Why, you are white, too!"

"Indeed I am. And I understand just how you feel. The other young elephants don't seem to like me either," sympathized Shamir. All of a sudden, Shamir had a wonderful idea.

"Would you like to go for a ride?" , he offered.

"I would love to!" laughed the monkey. "By the way, my name is Cheeku."

"And mine is Shamir."

And so the two of them proceeded together through the forest, laughing and chatting together. Each knew that he had found a friend.

Suddenly the two were startled by a loud trumpeting and the appearance of a huge bull elephant. The elephant moved beside them.

"Shamir, I am Simbu, your father," the great beast announced. "You have wandered too far away from the herd and are in great danger. All elephants are in danger where the catchers are present, but especially an elephant who is rare and white. Word has come that the king of Burma has sent his great elephant catcher, Lyling, to find white elephants for his herd. He is not far from this place right now. You must be very careful wherever you travel."

Simbu then led Shamir and his new friend Cheeku back to the herd. Maru rushed to greet him, then scolded him for wandering away. When she noticed the passenger on Shamir's back, his mother asked, "Who are you?"

"This is my friend Cheeku," responded Shamir in a protective tone.

Maru acknowledged the monkey and seemed happy that Shamir had found a friend.

Shamir turned to thank his father, but he had disappeared into the forest.

"When will he return, Mother?"

"When he is needed, Shamir," promised his mother.

And so Shamir and Cheeku played together that day and the next. They were inseparable. Cheeku had no family, so he joined the herd and lived with the elephants, spending much of his time on the back of Shamir.

One morning, some time later, Shamir awoke to find his friend missing.

Shamir sensed that his friend was in danger and, without thinking of the warning he had received so many times, he started off to look for Cheeku. (His mother and the other elephants were busy feeding upon the fruit trees and did not take notice of Shamir.)

In the distance, he could hear the faint cries of his friend. He ran toward that faint cry, not really paying much attention to where he was going. The herd was no longer in sight, but the cries of his friend were getting closer. At last, Shamir saw Cheeku, hanging from a tree branch, trying to pull himself free. As Shamir looked closer, he saw a rope knotted tightly around the leg of his friend. He was caught in a trap!

The trap had been set by Lyling, elephant catcher to the king of Burma. While Lyling was looking mainly for elephants, he also liked to take small monkeys to amuse the king. Cheeku would be considered a great treasure.

Shamir reached with his strong trunk into the tree and was able to snap the tree branch which held the rope. Cheeku fell a few short feet to the ground, loosened the rope, and was able to pull away.

Cheeku climbed on Shamir's back and the two friends started back in the direction of the herd.

8

Suddenly there was a loud breaking of tree branches and rolling of logs. Shamir found himself falling into a pit!

Lyling had been at work here too, and unless something happened soon, he would have a great prize, the rare white elephant, Shamir!

There was already the smell of Lyling in the air! There was not a minute to waste!

Cheeku, without hesitation started swinging through the trees swiftly. No monkey ever traveled faster than he as he flew through the air and back to the elephant herd. He quickly told Hannah what had happened.

Hannah trumpeted loudly and in only a moment both Maru and Simbu were at her side. Hannah told the rest of the herd to stay where they were and she and the other two elephants followed Cheeku to the place where Shamir was trapped.

They could not run, because Hannah knew there were other traps. She sniffed out each step, and Maru and Simbu stepped only where she stepped. Finally, the three elephants arrived at the pit where Shamir was trapped.

Shamir started to greet them with a loud trumpeting, but Hannah growled softly for him to be quiet. (Yes, elephants do growl.)

Hannah knew that the catcher was not far away.

She quickly located the edge of the pit and knelt there. The other elephants joined trunk and tail, and Simbu fastened his tail to a strong, slender tree. Then Hannah reached her long trunk down and Shamir stretched as far as he could and was just able to wrap his trunk around Hannah's. The three of them pulled, and Shamir scooted up the steep bank. In a short time, he was free.

There was no time to rejoice though, for Lyling riding his mighty elephant was sighted by Hannah.

"Follow me", signaled Hannah and the four elephants followed closely behind Hannah, again moving in single file,

9

stepping where she stepped. All knew that another pit could be waiting to trap one or more of them. But at last they reached the safety of the herd, far away from the catcher, Lyling.

Only then, did the elephants stop. At least for this day, they had won their freedom.

"Thank you for rescuing me," Shamir moved from one to the other of his family members, knowing that each had risked possible capture to save him.

"You too, Cheeku," he stroked the little monkey with his trunk.

"I'm sorry I caused so much trouble," Cheeku apologized.

"Never mind, little one, "said Hannah. We have all learned important lessons today. Perhaps these lessons will save us grief another day." All nodded in agreement.

The other young elephants gathered around Shamir and Cheeku, apologizing for their past behavior.

"We do want to play with you, Shamir," assured one of the young elephants.

"We are sorry we treated you so badly," apologized another.

"We would like to be friends with the monkey, Cheeku, too," announced a third.

Shamir gladly accepted the friendship offered to him. He looked at Cheeku and inquired if he agreed to accept the others.

Cheeku nodded his consent and all the young elephants and Cheeku started toward a clearing to play.

Simbu nudged Shamir and directed him toward Hannah and Maru.

"I must go away," said Simbu. "If you need me again, I will come."

He gave an affectionate stroke of his trunk to Shamir, then Maru, bowed respectfully to Hannah, and disappeared into the thick forest.

Hannah called the herd together to tell of their close call and announced that at first light they would be moving to another part of the forest, hoping to put greater distance between the herd and the mighty hunter. Meantime, they would eat, drink, and rest for their long journey.

Cheeku listened to the instructions given by the wise old elephant.

"May I go with you, Shamir?" the little monkey asked.

"Of course," replied Shamir. "You are a part of our family."

And so, at dawn, the herd of elephants led by Hannah, moved quietly through the forest. In the middle of the herd were several young elephants, now eager to be friends with one another regardless of color. In the very center was the white elephant, Shamir, and on his back was the small white monkey, Cheeku.

Hannah knew that they must move swiftly but with great caution. The trail of elephants was easy to find and the only safety was to keep moving. The wisdom of Hannah, and the obedience of the herd was their greatest assurance of safety.

This day, for this moment, they were safe from the great hunter. Tomorrow would bring new challenges and unforeseen dangers. However, now, as dawn breaks there is a contented sigh expressed as the herd lumbers toward a new place to feed, to play and to rest.

And so the two of them proceeded together through the forest, laughing and chatting together. Each knew that he had found a friend.

2

The Capture

The elephant herd had traveled for several days, stopping only long enough to eat and sleep. At last Hannah, the leader, trumpeted loudly and aimed her trunk triumphantly toward the place she had been seeking. It was a truly beautiful place. Small animals scurried through the brush. The trees hung heavy with lush vegetation, and the river was within eyesight and earshot of the clearing Hannah had chosen.

Hot and thirsty from their long trip, the herd moved immediately to the river, waded in and were soon playfully drinking and spraying one another with the cool refreshing water. Little Cheeku, the white monkey shrieked gleefully from Shamir's back as he found himself bathed in the cool liquid. The other elephant young joined in the game of water tag and mud hats, seeing how large a pack they could hold on their large heads. In the mud hat game, Shamir was the undisputed winner. He trumpeted loudly as he was crowned the champion unanimously by the playful group. Cheeku shrieked his approval and jumped from the back of one elephant to another, patting each fondly as he leapt about. As last all were sufficiently played out and lumbered back to the shore for feasting and a long nap.

What the herd did not know, not even the wise and wily Hannah, was that they were being tracked from afar by Lyling, the great elephant catcher from the court of King Burengdong of Burma. Lyling had spied the white elephant from afar as the herd fled from the near capture of Shamir, and had spent several months preparing to capture the white elephant and bring the rare prize to his King. The fact that the herd was in the forests of India did not deter him. He traveled almost alone, on the back of his favorite "koonkie," a trained elephant, who was called Sheba. Only his young servant boy, Absom, and his young elephant, Lena, accompanied Lyling. Remaining upstream and keeping their distance, the small party had managed to elude detection. If he were bent upon capturing an entire herd, traveling alone would have been foolish. However, Lyling had only one prize in mind, the white elephant, Shamir.

Lyling spied cautiously upon the vast herd. Hannah, the female elephants and the young were directly across the shallow, narrow bend in the river only a short distance downstream. The male elephants lagged a mile or more behind, close enough to keep in touch, but maintaining their necessary space. Lyling would have to develop a plan to lure the white elephant away from the others. After that, capture would be easy. He did not guess that the plot would accidentally involve Shamir's friend, the monkey, Cheeku.

It was the heat of the afternoon and all the elephants were resting. Some were lying down, but most merely stood, sleeping. Cheeku was restless and whispered to Shamir that a walk in the forest would be nice. Shamir was a bit sleepy, but decided to oblige his friend.

15

"Okay, but just a short one. I don't want to go too far away from the herd."

"Of course," Cheeku agreed. "I just want to see if I can find a monkey or two."

Shamir was sympathetic to Cheeku's needs. While he loved living with the elephant herd, sometimes Cheeku became lonesome for his own kind. Perhaps they could find a playmate for him. Even though Shamir was now almost six years old, he was still young and lacking in judgment. His interest in finding a playmate for Cheeku, was to deliver him right into the hands of the enemy.

As the two friends walked by the river, Cheeku heard the cries of monkeys across the water. With only a little urging, Shamir walked into the river and began swimming to the other side. At this point, the river was narrow, only about 300 feet wide, and easily crossed. The two friends emerged from the water again cooled and refreshed and listened carefully to determine the origin of the screeching monkey cries.

"That way!" Cheeku pointed upstream. Shamir nodded and started toward the cries.

As the two began making their way upstream, Lyling and Absom were dosing lazily only a few yards away. They might have missed the opportunity altogether had not Lena chosen to trumpet loudly, signaling the presence of the two. Lyling opened his eyes and watched in amazement as his selected prey edged closer.

At this moment, Cheeku found the group of monkeys playing together in the trees. These monkeys did not reject him, but were rather friendly and beckoned to him to come and play. He left the back of Shamir and swung toward the playful monkeys. Soon, he was out of sight enjoying the afternoon with his new friends. His absence made the planned capture almost a certainty.

Shamir decided to catch a few winks of sleep while his friend played. He moved in the shade of a large banyan tree and napped peacefully.

Lyling, riding Sheba, and Absom, on the back of Lena moved quietly toward the young white elephant. The noose was slipped around his neck and one elephant and rider were on each side as he wakened. Though he was startled and trumpeted loudly, there was nothing Shamir could do. He was being led away, firmly noosed and held by the powerful koonkie, Sheba, assisted by the young elephant, Lena, and the boy, Absom. They were moving quickly away from his herd and away from Shamir's friend, Cheeku. He was frightened but Shamir had no choice but to go where he was being lead, otherwise the noose would choke him.

Cheeku heard the trumpeting, but chose to ignore it. He thought Shamir was only telling him it was time to go. He was not ready to leave. He had found several new friends, among them a lovely female monkey named Meela. He might just have to stay here for a few hours or maybe even a few days. By the time he decided to go back and tell Shamir that he was going to stay with his new friends for awhile, Shamir was gone.

"I guess he got tired of waiting," thought Cheeku. "He must have gone home without me. Maru probably called him. I am sure he will come back for me later."

Though he felt some uneasiness, his pleasure at finding his new friends overcame his doubts and he went back to join them.

In the meantime, Maru awakened and called for her son. When he did not answer, she began to search for him among the other young elephants.

"Have you seen Shamir?" She asked each friend, growing more frantic with each negative response. She had also noted that Cheeku was missing as well. She

17

instinctively knew that where one was, the other was probably there as well.

At last one of the older elephants came to her side to tell her what she had seen earlier in the day. "I don't really know where he is now, Maru, but I do know that I saw him leave with Cheeku some time ago. Most of the herd was sleeping. Just as I was dozing off, I saw Shamir and Cheeku cross the river, right over there." She motioned to the narrow bend in the river where the two friends had last been seen.

Maru thanked her friend for the information and swiftly entered the river. As she reached the other side a short time later, she trumpeted loudly, signaling danger.

Cheeku heard the persistent trumpeting and recognized the call of distress. He quickly moved to the shore where Maru was emerging from the water.

Maru looked relieved when she saw Cheeku.

"Cheeku, I've been looking everywhere for Shamir. Do you know where he is?"

Cheeku bowed his head in shame. "I left him standing right here."

"When, Cheeku, WHEN?" Maru sounded frightened.

Cheeku watched the sun setting in the western sky. "It was several hours ago. I asked him to bring me over to play with these new friends," he gestured toward Meela who had followed him to the clearing.. "I thought he had gone home without me when he wasn't here a couple of hours ago."

"Shamir is missing, Cheeku," Maru confirmed his fear. "No one has seen him since he crossed the river with you early in the afternoon."

"Cheeku bowed his head and covered his eyes. Once again he had been responsible for placing his friend in danger.

Just then a large bull elephant entered the clearing. It was Simbu, Shamir's father.

"I have bad news, Maru." A herd of elephants just passed this way. They said that a young white elephant was seen captured and being led away by Lyling, the elephant catcher. They are several hours ahead, downstream. I'm afraid he is lost to us. There is little we can do to get him back."

Maru wept. She loved her beautiful son. He was still several years away from living on his own. Her only consolation was that she had heard that King Burengnong treated his white elephants well. Shamir would not be harmed. Besides, Maru was expecting another elephant calf. It was due in only a few short months. She could not look back but must rather look ahead. She would grieve for her son and miss him all her life long, but she had to go on.

Simbu joined trunks with Maru then stroked her gently. "I am so sorry, Maru. I would try to chase them, but I am afraid it would be fruitless."

Maru nodded in agreement and the two elephants walked into the river and swam to the other side where the rest of the herd waited for news.

Hannah, the wise old leader of the herd, and grandmother of Shamir also wept for the missing white elephant. She admitted that chasing after him would be useless.

"Only a miracle would return him to us," she sighed as she stroked Maru's head and back.

He was being led away, firmly noosed and held by the powerful koonkie, Sheba, assisted by the young elephant, Lena, and the boy, Absom.

3

The Long Journey

As Shamir moved reluctantly with his captors, the boy, Absom spoke gently to him.

"It is going to be all right, little one. The king is proud of his white elephants and takes very good care of them. You will be the youngest and the most beautiful. Perhaps I will become your Mahout (trainer). I will ask the young prince. He is a friend of mine." The gentle voice of the boy soothed the spirit of Shamir.

Absom was lean and well muscled for a boy of twelve years. His smile was warm and his touch firm but gentle as he sought to ease the fears of Shamir. It was obvious that he cared about the elephant, not just as a commodity to bring gold, but as a creature of the wild, worthy of being loved and cared for.

Lena, Absom's young elephant, also spoke quietly to Shamir. "Do not be afraid, my friend. Absom is the kindest of boys. When you are sad, he will sing you songs to chase away your unhappiness. He will stroke you and feed you, and see that you are well cared for. Besides, it will be nice to have a playmate. I am the only young elephant in the royal stables. I hope we can be friends."

Shamir immediately liked this beautiful young elephant. She did not seem to mind at all that he was white. He sensed that she would help make his captivity bearable.

Lyling was an experienced catcher, the finest in Burma. His voice was stern and he was all business. He respected the wild animals he captured, but his love was in the chase, the domination, and the glory and recognition. It was important to him that he be the best at what he did and the accolades received from the king and court proved he had been successful. He had sharp eyes, steady and skillful hands, and the ability to lead his koonkie, Sheba, to places other elephants feared to go. Though he led Sheba, into many dangerous places, his bravery and confidence made her eager and ready to obey, whatever the consequences. Thus far, they had been an indomitable team.

The trail from the mouth of the Ganges into Burma was a long and arduous journey. It was also dangerous when you were taking with you a small white elephant, sacred to the religions of both India and Burma. Usually, the safest route would be to follow the roadway by the sea to the mouth of the Sittang River, then upstream to the city, Toungoo, the capital city. Instead, where the river widened to form the eastern mouth of the Ganges, the small party turned toward the East, choosing an overland route through treacherous country.

The route away from the sea toward the Chin Hills of Burma, was not the easiest journey, but Lyling was forced to make this choice due to an unfortunate event along the way.

22

The trouble started when they edged close to the seaport town of what is now Chittagong, in order to pick up some supplies for their journey to Burma.. Absom had been left with the elephants, while Lyling went into the village to purchase some essentials for their journey to Toungoo, then the capital and home of the King of Burma. To keep from arousing suspicion, he decided to go on foot surmising that he could carry all the necessary supplies. Shamir was tied firmly to a tree and hidden in some thick shrubbery while Absom kept watch over the elephants. As he waited alone, he was approached by a band of strangers. There were three men and two elephants. He recognized from the ropes they carried and the movement of their elephants that they, too, were elephant catchers. Though he pretended not to understand their language, he knew much of what they were saying They spoke of Lyling and his reputation as a great catcher. A man they called "Kasha" seemed to be the leader. He recognized Sheba, the favorite koonkie of Lyling who accompanied him on catching expeditions. Though looking for elephants in other territories was generally not a problem since elephants were quite plentiful everywhere, bagging a prize white elephant and removing it from the country could be extremely dangerous. Luckily for Absom, the catchers did not see the white elephant hidden in the shrubbery, covered by blankets to hide his color. They did wonder why Lyling was here, at the mouth of the Ganges with this young boy and two elephants.

As Absom continued to listen, pretending to understand nothing, he discovered that Kasha the head of the party was the great elephant catcher from the court of Akbar, Emperor of the Mogul Kingdom of India. Kasha, too, had heard rumors of a white elephant in the area. A catcher was always richly rewarded by a ruler for bringing a white elephant to his stable. He wondered what Lyling knew and where he might be going. Kasha suggested to his friends

23

that they go into town and search for Lyling. One catcher was left to watch Absom, while the others went to find Lyling, gather reinforcements and prepare to follow the Lyling party if they discovered that he knew anything of the white elephant. Absom was frightened but acted as though he understood nothing.

In a short time, Lyling returned from his errands. Realizing that they were in eyesight of Kasha's spy, Absom quickly explained what had happened. Knowing they had little time to waste, Lyling told Absom that they must leave immediately. While the spy watched from afar, the man and the boy mounted the two elephants, went to the thick brush, untied a third elephant, and began to run toward the Chin Hills of Burma Even though the young elephant was covered, it was still evident that he was white!

The spy knew he could do no good alone, so instead of chasing them, he mounted his elephant and rode toward the village to find his friends.

Lyling knew that Kasha and his party would be trailing them. He also knew that their greatest chance to succeed was in getting Shamir into Burma then traveling through the Chin Hills. While Kasha had often been to Burma, he always took the river route. He did not know the way through the Chin Hills. These were the hills where Lyling had been born and played and learned to hunt and trap animals. He knew each path and obstacle. The journey would be difficult for him, but treacherous and extremely dangerous for Kasha. This would be Lyling's escape route.

Kasha and his party saw their friend riding toward them with the news. Lyling was heading out of the country and he had with him a young white elephant! The spy motioned toward the direction they had headed. This had puzzled him because he always traveled with Kasha following the sea.

Kasha gathered his party together and prepared to head for Burma.

"I know where he is going," Kasha acknowledged. "Perhaps we can head him off before he reaches the capital city. After that, there will be too great a danger The king will have troops everywhere."

Lyling and Absom drove their small party on through the night. They wanted to reach the hills where following them would be difficult for Kasha. Lyling knew of narrow trails through the hills that would be difficult for a large party to follow. Still, he recognized that they were in great danger until they were almost to the city of Toungoo. The thick brush and gnarled pathways would lead them to the shores of the Irrawaddy River which they would cross then travel the lowlands several miles to Toungoo, their destination.

Lyling thought that Kasha and his party would turn back when they saw the difficulty in following them. He was right in thinking they would not follow them. He was wrong in thinking they would turn back. Kasha had another scheme in mind.

The man, the boy and the three elephants trudged on. They were never sure that they were safe. Shamir was lonely and sad to be away from his family. He missed his mother and his friend, Cheeku. However, he was calmed and comforted by the soothing words of Absom and the sweet songs as well.

> *"Beautiful elephant, born by the river, a rain*
> *forest baby so white,*
> *Though you've left the Ganges, you'll love your*
> *new home,*
> *Always safe, never out of my sight."*

(These were not the exact words, but this is what the song meant.)

Shamir discovered that Sheba and Lena were mother and daughter and they had been in captivity for several years, since Lena was very small. They had also come from the shores of the Ganges River. Sheba sensed that Shamir missed his mother and tried to treat him as she thought Maru would have treated him. Lena was like the big sisters and cousins who had helped care for Shamir in his herd. Both Sheba and Lena were kind to him and assured Shamir that he would be well cared for.

"In fact, Shamir, you will have little work to do, " Lena noted in mock jealousy. "You will carry the king or prince occasionally, and march in parades, and be displayed for others to admire. You will never have to be a koonkie and catch other elephants, or build houses, or work in any way."

"Why is that?", asked Shamir.

"Because you are white, and that makes you sacred and very important," Lena explained

"That is very strange," Shamir observed, "When I was very young everyone hated me because I was white; everyone except my mother and grandmother, of course. They loved me and then..." he paused haltingly, "there was Cheeku. He loved me, too."

Shamir found himself telling his new friends how he had met the white monkey and rescued him from the monkeys who were beating him. He also told them how Cheeku had helped save him from the pit. He wondered where Cheeku was now. He knew he must be very sad that Shamir was gone. Had Cheeku stayed with the monkeys they had found on the other side of the River, or had he returned to his adopted elephant family? Wherever he was, Shamir missed Cheeku very much.

What Shamir did not know was that his friend was only a few miles from him at that very moment.

At last the party could hear the waters of the Irrawaddy River. Perched high on the hills, they could see the people, animals and boats below. Lyling scanned the river area looking for the best way to leave the hills and cross the

Irrawaddy River. Through the corner of his eye he saw something unexpected and a cause for grave concern. It was Kasha and his party waiting at the water's edge keeping watch for Lyling and the white elephant. Lyling motioned to Absom to move back into the heavily forested area. Their arrival in Toungoo would have to be delayed a few more days because they would have to move overland for several more miles before crossing the river.

Kasha and his men had boarded a sea vessel and traveled by water from the sea and upstream into the place where he knew the mountain passage led, just north of Pagan, the ancient capital. The plan was to capture Shamir here at the Irrawaddy and carry him by boat back to India. Kasha had not counted on being detected by Lyling. While the Kasha party waited below, Lyling and Absom wound their way toward the city of Prome, following the Irrawaddy River but staying several hundred yards back until they reached the edge of the city. They crossed the river and made their way overland to the edge of the city Toungoo. When the King's troops were in sight to protect them, the small group entered the city. There was proud Lyling on the back of Sheba, Absom, riding Lena, and the beautiful white elephant walking between Lena and Sheba. A large crowd of people followed them right to the steps of the palace. The people clapped and cheered as King Burengnong and his attendants met them at the palace door.

"Good work, Lyling!" he congratulated the catcher. "You shall be richly rewarded for your capture of this sacred beast."

Absom bowed to the king and to the prince, who was also his friend.

"I have made friends with this elephant, your Majesty. I would consider it a great honor to become his mahout.

The king looked skeptical. "You are only a boy. It is a big responsibility to train the king's white elephant."

27

"I know sir. However, my father has trained many elephants for the king, including his prize white elephant who recently died. He will help me. This young elephant likes me. He will respond to me, I am sure."

"I agree, my father," chimed in the prince. Absom has grown up with elephants. He will be a wonderful mahout for the white one."

The king finally agreed and Absom took the new prize to the special stables reserved for animals belonging to the king. Shamir was frightened but also excited. He did not know what was in store for him in this new life, but it was sure to be an exciting adventure.

As Shamir was taken to the King's stable, Kasha and his men looked on from afar. They had discovered too late that the party had gone another way and were safe inside the gates of the city. It looked as though they would have to return home without the white elephant.

However, Kasha did not give up easily. Perhaps they would stay close by and wait for another opportunity.

As he waited alone, he was approached by a band of strangers . . . He recognized from the ropes they carried and the movement of their elephants that they, too, were elephant catchers.

4

Cheeku's Adventure

As Cheeku spoke with the Maru and Hannah about the disappearance of Shamir, he could see the ache and hurt in their eyes and in their hearts. It was no less than the feelings he had for his special friend.   There was one difference. He could travel through the trees much faster than they could move. Perhaps he could at least find Shamir and see that he was cared for. He even had visions of rescuing him, though he did not really know how at this moment.   He only knew that he must try to find out what had happened.

He bade farewell to his elephant family and promised to keep in touch. He did not tell them that he was going to seek Shamir. They would have discouraged him from such a dangerous journey. However, as he swung away through the trees, Maru knew how much Cheeku loved Shamir, and she instinctively knew that he was going to try to find him.

As Cheeku made his way through the jungle, he realized that he would need help in picking up the trail. "Excuse me, please," he interrupted the chattering of a group of

Hanuman langurs, the same family of monkeys he belonged to. "I am looking for my friend, a white elephant. Word is that he was captured by an elephant catcher. I must find him."

The monkeys stopped their chattering and stared at the monkey.

"You are certainly a strange looking creature! Why should we help you?" they asked.

"Because, I am a monkey just like you. I need your help." Cheeku replied, desperately.

"Besides, he is my friend," said a voice from behind.

It was his friend, Meela! She had been following him.

"Cheeku is a kind and caring monkey. The fact that he looks a little different has nothing to do with that. How many of you would leave your home and travel alone just to see if a friend is all right? " Meela had made a good point and the monkeys looked a bit ashamed.

Finally, one of them spoke. "As a matter of fact, they did come this way and were heading for the eastern mouth of the Ganges. There were two catchers, the great Lyling and a young boy who traveled with him. They rode two elephants, a large one and a younger one. The white one you speak of was between them with a noose around his neck."

"Thank you very much," Shamir and Meela replied in chorus.

"Let's go!" shouted Meela. "There is not a minute to lose."

"But Meela, this is a very dangerous journey. I wouldn't want to see you hurt," objected Cheeku.

"I want to go with you, and you will get more cooperation if you take me with you. Don't argue, Cheeku. You need all the help you can get." Meela was obviously very determined.

She was right of course. He would have to explain to everyone without her. With her, they could receive help immediately and without argument. It should not be so, but it was true.

Cheeku had to admit, he would be happy to have the company of the beautiful, Meela. She had already stolen his heart in only a few short hours. Traveling with her would make the difficult journey much more pleasant.

Meela and Cheeku traveled rapidly through the forest, swinging from tree to tree, asking for information when the trail grew cold. As they reached the eastern mouth of the Ganges where it flowed into the ocean, they lost the trail. No one seemed to know which way they were going or where they might look. As they looked toward the south, they saw ships sailing in both directions. The west led through the city of Chittagong, toward Calcutta. Since they had just come from the north they could not imagine that was where they might go. As they looked to the east, the Chin Hills of Burma rose before them.

"That would be a difficult way to travel," Cheeku was thinking aloud.

"It doesn't mean that is not the way they would be going, though," Meela added.

They paused for a few minutes to think about what their next step would be. They munched on wild fruit in the swampy area and rested briefly. As they observed the people at the edge of the city, several men and elephants came into view. They watched the men talking to a young boy who stood beside a large elephant and a smaller one. While the boy looked like the one described by the monkeys who had led them to this place, and the other two elephants also fit the descriptions, Shamir was nowhere to be seen. They were curious and continued to observe the scenario being played out before them.

The three men spoke to the boy for a few moments then two of them hurriedly mounted their elephants and headed toward town. The other man sat several yards away from the boy and seemed to be watching him. Another man appeared on foot carrying two large baskets. The boy ran to meet him and spoke to him The man quickly placed the baskets on the back of the large elephant. The boy and the man ran toward a tree surrounded by heavy brush and emerged leading another elephant. This elephant was almost completely covered with a large blanket. However, there was no mistaking it. The elephant was young and definitely white!

"That is him!," exclaimed Cheeku. "That is Shamir!"

"What do we do now?" asked Meela.

"We follow them." answered Cheeku. "We must keep our distance though. We won't be much help if we get caught, too."

And so the two of them kept the fleeing party in sight and followed closely enough to keep from losing the trail, but far enough to remain unseen.

The trail they followed was through the Chin Hills. The hills were thick with trees and mountain streams. The trail seemed so narrow at times they suspected that Lyling was blazing his own trail. It was not difficult for the tree swinging monkeys but they suspected it must be very difficult for the three lumbering elephants.

Sometimes, when the party stopped to rest, they would move in closely to their camp. However, they were afraid to speak to Shamir. They were afraid they might startle him and give themselves away. They also suspected that the wily Lyling might take a fancy to the white monkey and try to capture him as well. It certainly would not be the first time. Cheeku remembered an earlier time when he escaped the trap only through the aide of his friend Shamir.

34

"The boy seems to like Shamir," observed Meela. "He sings to him and talks to him as they walk. If one must be in captivity, it is good to have a friend who is kind and will look after you."

Cheeku agreed.

The two monkeys followed the party to the edge of the Chin Hills. They expected them to go down to the water and follow the river to their destination. They were puzzled when Lyling said something to the boy and the three of them disappeared once again into the thickly forested hills.

Cheeku and Meela did not understand these movements because they did not see Kasha and his men waiting by the river. However, they did not question the movements they merely followed.

A few days later, they saw the party enter into the city, followed by many people, laughing and singing and bowing toward Lyling and the elephants.

"Look, Cheeku," exclaimed Meela, "Aren't those the same men we saw just before we discovered Shamir."

"You are right, Meela. I'll bet they are up to no good." Cheeku shuddered. "Now we will have to be careful not to be seen by them either."

The men kept their distance from Lyling and his prize. However, their eyes did not leave Shamir even once.

"I must make contact with Shamir, soon," resolved Cheeku. "He needs to know what he is up against."

"But how?" asked Meela. "I don't know, yet. I only know it is very important."

The two sat in a high tree overlooking the city, developing a plan to help Shamir, realizing that the problems were now doubled and any thought of rescue was probably wishful thinking.

"There must be a way," Cheeku exclaimed. However, his tone was not hopeful.

35

"Cheeku is a kind and caring monkey. The fact that he looks a little different has nothing to do with that. How many of you would leave your home and travel alone just to see if a friend is all right?" Meela had made a good point and the monkeys looked a bit ashamed.

5

The Royal Elephant

"More Precious Than Gold"

As Meela had remarked when she saw Absom caressing Shamir, "If you must be in captivity, it is good to have someone who cares for you."

It was certainly true that Absom cared a great deal for Shamir. Each morning he came to the stable and saw that Shamir was fed and clean. In a few weeks, he was ready to ride Shamir.

"Do not be afraid, I will guide you gently. I will not hurt you. However, you must learn to bear the weight of not only one man but two, and a special carriage they will also place on you, when either the prince or the king are riding. I am the only other one allowed to ride you," Absom announced proudly.

Absom then moved to Lena who was always at Shamir's side to show him the way. "Watch carefully. Lena and I will show you."

Shamir watched as Absom stood upon a high stool and climbed on Lena's back. He sat forward on the elephant, almost at her neck. His feet rested behind Lena's ears. He then slid off Lena's back and moved toward Shamir.

"Your turn, Shamir," whispered Absom softly, stroking Shamir's trunk, and humming soothingly.

This time the high stool was next to Shamir and soon Absom was sitting on Shamir's back. He moved carefully into the spot right behind Shamir's ears. Soon it was clear to Shamir why Absom's feet rested behind his ears. With his feet pressed behind Shamir's ears, Absom guided him in the direction he wanted him to go, signaled him when to stop and start, and when to go faster or slow down. Absom also spoke to him firmly punctuating the directions he gave. Shamir was startled at first, but he soon caught on as to what was expected of him. The boy was heavier than Cheeku, but he was used to having a friend on his back to share conversation and exploration. He was happy to have the company and Absom was a wonderful singer with a warm and friendly laugh. Shamir liked him very much.

Besides, Lena was always at his side, ready to encourage him, to show him what to do, and talk to him when he felt sad. She always seemed to understand. He still missed his family in the wild, but he had to admit that he was given all the food he wanted and he was never alone.

The king saw to it that the stable containing his white elephants was carefully guarded. To the king, his white elephants were more precious than gold. Both Shamir and an older white elephant, Kordo, were treated as sacred beasts. Buddhists believe that white elephants bring good luck and in the Hindu religion, a white elephant named Airavata is considered the ancestor of all elephants, having been born from the churning seas. Therefore, when a rare white elephant is captured, it is treated with respect and carefully guarded.

38

Shamir tried hard to please Absom. He realized that Absom's success would mean he could continue to train the white elephant. Since Absom was very kind to him, he believed it would be much better to be his is capable hands than in those of one who might treat him cruelly.

One day Absom worked especially hard with Shamir. He put a special kind of saddle on him and had Shamir practice carrying someone in the saddle. Absom seemed very excited. "Tomorrow you will be in the parade. On your back will be the prince, my friend, Risha. You must walk proudly but be very careful. The prince is very precious cargo."

Shamir had met Prince Risha. He had often come to the stable to help Absom. When he came, there were many guards around, and they watched, unsmiling, while the two boys, Absom and Risha laughed and played. There was never any privacy. Both the prince and Shamir were too valuable to leave alone.

As Absom said good night to Shamir, he whispered softly to him. "You have worked very hard, White One. I will be here first thing in the morning to practice with you."

Shamir did not understand all that was going on, but he realized that it would be a very important day. The guards and the stable keepers all seemed a little on edge. Everyone seemed to feel that their positions and being in favor with the king depended on Shamir's performance.

Back in the stable, he asked his friend, Lena, what all the fuss was about. Even though she was not a white elephant, Lena was in the stable right next to Shamir because she was helping with the training. Shamir was very relieved and happy that she was there. Old Kordo, the white elephant was cross and seemed very jealous of the attention Shamir was getting.

"If you do not do well, all of them will be blamed for any mistakes you make. Also, they must continue to guard you and that is much more difficult in the parade," Lena explained. "Their lives may even depend on your doing well."

The young elephant resolved to do as his best. He had difficulty sleeping as he planned every move he would make as he carried the young prince. Long after the rest of the stable slept, he was still awake, thinking about tomorrow.

Suddenly, Shamir was startled by a whisper from the dark corner of his stable.

"Shamir, move over this way, but don't make any fast moves. You might waken the guards. It is me, Cheeku."

Shamir was so excited he almost panicked. Realizing that noise would put his friends in danger, he controlled his joy at hearing from Cheeku and whispered softly, "How did you find me? Are you all right? "

From his dark corner of the stable Cheeku assured Shamir that he was just fine. He told him how he and Meela had followed their party through the Chin Hills and into Toungoo.

"I am concerned, Shamir. Lyling is not the only catcher who wants you. Kasha from the Mogul kingdom of India has also followed you right into Toungoo. He has been here for the several weeks you have been here. Afraid to go home empty handed, he is looking for an opportunity to snatch you and take you back with him. At least here, you have the young boy who looks after you. Kasha seems cruel and merciless. I am not so sure he would care for you the way they do here," Cheeku warned.

"My dear friend, Cheeku, you were so kind to follow me here. Now, you and Meela must return to the forest. Find my family. Tell them I am being treated well but miss them all very much. If there is anyway to return to them someday, I will."

Cheeku jumped gently onto the back of Shamir, a place where he had spent so many happy hours. He stroked the

40

neck and head of his friend then whispered, "Good-bye, Shamir, I hope we will meet again someday. Meanwhile, I will do as you say. I will carry news back to your family."

Shamir's eyes were wet with tears as the monkey leapt into the darkness and out of the stable.

"What is that noise?" One of the guards carried a lamp and brought it into Shamir's stable.

When he saw that Shamir was shivering and damp, he put a blanket on his back. "Have a bad dream, did you little White One? Don't worry, everything will be all right." He patted Shamir and left with the lamp. Shamir was again in darkness and Cheeku was on his way back home.

At least, that is where he was headed along with his friend, Meela. Shamir desperately hoped they would make the journey safely. As Cheeku swung through the trees to join Meela, the full moon lighted his way. The moonlight also made it possible for Kasha, hiding outside the stable, to see the white monkey. As Meela and Cheeku left the forested area outside the stable and headed for the eastern shores of the Ganges, they were not alone. One of Kasha's men mounted his elephant and was not far behind.

The next morning Absom came to prepare Shamir for the processional. "Today, you will be the center of attention. I will be riding you as usual, but behind me will be Prince Risha. He is proud to be riding you. His father will be on the old white elephant, Kordo. I'm afraid Kordo has been in a bad mood lately, but he seemed all right this morning. I hope everything goes well.

Shamir was covered in blankets of fine silks and linens. A special saddle, covered with gold and silver that looked somewhat like a lantern with open windows was placed on his back along with a large velvet pillow. Risha was lifted on behind Absom, placed on the pillow, and the three of them took their place in the royal processional. There were four guards in front, four in back of Shamir, and two on

41

each side, all dressed in handsome red uniforms trimmed in gold. They wore white turbans on their heads and carried large jeweled swords. It was quite an impressive looking group.

The king was behind them dressed in fine splendor with a larger, more opulent version of Prince Risha. There were six guards in front, six behind, and four on each side. They were also dressed in the same finery as Prince Risha's guards.

The streets were lined with the townspeople. All wanted to catch a glance of King Burengnong, Prince Risha, and the sacred white elephants. The king and the prince waved and the crowds bowed respectfully and cheered.

Among the townspeople, observing the spectacle, were Kasha, great elephant catcher from the Mogul Kingdom of India and his men.

Shamir was covered in blankets of fine silks and linens. . . . .Risha was lifted on behind Absom, placed on a pillow, and the three of them took their place in the royal procession.

6

A Dangerous Route Back Home

As Meela and Cheeku began to wind their way back through the Forest, they realized that they were being followed by a catcher on his elephant.

"It is one of Kasha's men!" shrieked Cheeku. "I recognize him from the our earlier meeting. He must have seen me leave the stable after talking with Shamir."

"What shall we do, Cheeku?" asked Meela. "How do we throw him off the trail.."

"We will do exactly as Lyling and his party did in coming here. We will take the rugged route through the Chin Hills. That is the way we came here. The trails are narrow and difficult to follow. I believe we can lose him."

The two monkeys swung swiftly through the trees, moving close to the trail made by Lyling and Absom, but never getting too close, hoping to avoid detection by Machi, Kasha's assistant.

Machi, meanwhile, lost the monkeys on one occasion, but accidentally discovered the trail made by the three elephants when they cut their way through the hills to avoid Kasha's party. While it was largely overgrown, to the practiced eye of a catcher, the trail was still evident.

"No wonder we lost them," remarked Machi. "However, I now know just how to travel through these hills. The monkeys may get there first, but I will catch up with them."

Machi did not know why the white monkey had come out of the stable, but he suspected it had something to do with Shamir. "Strange as it may seem," he thought, "The white monkey and the white elephant might be friends. Perhaps the color of their skin brought them together."

A white monkey is extremely rare in the wild. Without protection, such as that given Cheeku by his friend Shamir, they are often scorned by their own kind and die. Thus far, Cheeku had been lucky. First he had Shamir, and now he had Meela. Both had learned to love the monkey for his good heart, courageous spirit and cheerful disposition. They had kept others from hurting him.

However, the same coloring that made Cheeku peculiar and unacceptable to other monkeys, was also the reason he was now being chased by Machi. Monkeys were entertaining in the king's court. There were several trained monkeys who amused the ruler and his guests. A rare white monkey would be a real prize. He and his friend could be trained to beg, to dance, to do tricks, and be dressed up and sent out to amuse their guests. While a white monkey would be no substitute for a white elephant, he would be a valued consolation prize if they did not capture the white elephant, and a welcome additional catch if they did.

For several days, Machi followed the pair, sleeping only when they slept, and moving quickly on the trail blazed by Lyling a few weeks before. Finally, he was back at

Chittagong, at the eastern mouth of the Ganges. Here Machi picked up fresh supplies and a servant to help him keep on the trail. They were far more likely to follow the trail if one of them was alert at all times. That is how Meela and Cheeku had managed to stay far ahead of them, by taking turns sleeping and guarding. Still, elephants, monkeys and people all needed rest sometimes. Elephants also had to stop along the way to eat the 500 pounds of food they usually consume each day. The monkeys moved faster and the hunters grew further behind.

At last, the monkeys arrived at the place in the river where Shamir had been captured. They looked all around for Hannah and the elephant herd. No elephants were in sight.

Meela suggested that they find her family and see if they had any news. The two monkeys moved to the place where they had first met. The trees were still thick with Meela's friends and family. When they saw Meela, they grew very excited and chattered joyously.

"Meela, we've missed you. We were so afraid you would never come back to us." They noticed that Cheeku was at her side. "I see you still have your friend, the white monkey, with you."

"Cheeku is my friend. In fact, Cheeku and I are expecting a family in the spring," announced Meela proudly.

"Congratulations, Meela, and to you also, Cheeku," offered Meela's mother. She turned to one of the others and whispered, "I hope the baby looks like Meela instead of Cheeku."

"I heard that, Mother," chided Meela. "I don't care who our child looks like. I only hope he or she has the heart of Cheeku. He is brave and as loyal a friend as one could have. What a monkey has inside is far more important than how he looks."

"I know you are right, Meela," her mother agreed, bowing her head in shame. "I was just thinking about the way those who look so different are treated."

"If YOU treat others kindly, then you will set an example for others," suggested Meela.

"You are so wise, my daughter," sighed Mother. "Since you were a wee one, you have been full of the wisdom of one much older. May you serve as an example to all of us."

Cheeku hugged Meela proudly. "You are the finest mate one could have."

"And so are you, Cheeku," added Meela.

"And now, we really need your help," Cheeku pleaded. "We are looking for Shamir's family. We promised Shamir that we would try to find them and tell them that he is safe. He is in captivity, but he has a young trainer, a Mahout, who takes good care of him."

The monkeys chattered with each other, asking throughout the area if any had seen Shamir's family. The message echoed throughout the forest. Meela and Cheeku were seeking information on Hannah, the Matriarch, and her herd. It took several hours, but at last an old and wise monkey, Ramsa, swung through the trees and rested beside the pair.

Meela recognized the old monkey. "Uncle Ramsa! How good to see you. Can you help us find Hannah and the elephant herd."

The old monkey nodded. "I have seen the herd. They are on this side of the Ganges, several miles upstream. The food supply was not adequate and they had to move on."

"Thank you, Ramsa. We must go quickly and find them. Shamir asked that we find them and take back word of his safety, even though he is in captivity." Cheeku did not wish to be rude to the wise old monkey, but he was anxious to move on.

"Wait, my friend. Before you go, you should know that all has not gone well with the herd since Shamir was captured."

"What do you mean, Ramsa? Please, what happened?"

Ramsa explained quickly what had happened. Evidently the spotting of a white elephant had brought catchers from everywhere. The herd seemed always to be on the run. The food supply had also been dwindling making it necessary to keep moving. They had been on the move a few weeks before, when the disaster had occurred.

The old monkey nodded. "I have seen the herd. They are on this side of the Ganges, several miles upstream. The food supply was not adequate and they had to move on."

7

The Khedda

"Hasti! Hasti!"

Hannah and the herd had found the food supply
dwindling and had decided to move. They felt that Shamir
was lost to them forever. No one ever seemed to return
from captivity. Hannah, as always, made the decision to
move on. Their herd was a large one: fifty elephants when
the twenty young elephants were included. Maru had just
given birth to a female calf she had named Cali. Others had
new calves as well. They would need more food.

Years ago, Hannah had been across the Ganges upstream
several miles. She remembered lush vegetation in addition
to the adequate water supply. There was also grassland,
easier for the elephants to move. At first, she hesitated to
take them this route, because they were much easier to
sight. However, the situation was becoming desperate, and
she believed it would be necessary to move quickly.

They had crossed the river and had traveled several miles north. Hannah had located the clearing and the herd was making good time as they traveled through a narrow patch of grassland.

Because of the narrowness of the clearing, the herd was strung out. Hannah had asked one of her sisters, Emma, to bring up the rear of the herd to watch for danger. The herd was, in reality, so stretched out that it was almost like two herds. At one point, one of the females traveling with Emma found it was time to give birth to a new calf. While the birth was not difficult, it still took at least two hours before she and her new calf were ready to travel again. As approximately ten elephants and about a dozen young elephants ranging in age from two months to eight years, fell back with Emma, the rest of the herd moved on, unaware of the problem. The females assisted the new mother and their young ones played, happy for a chance to nibble without being pushed on.

Hannah was intent on looking for pits and watching for catchers or hunters at the front. She was unaware that Emma was delayed at the rear. Besides, an elephant's sense of smell is very good. If a small separation occurred, the scent would not be lost and the stragglers could catch up.

As Emma helped with the new birth she knew that her group would be dragging behind. She asked one of her older sons, Jaku, to run ahead and tell the rest of the herd that they would be delayed due to the birth. Emma knew that when the word reached Hannah, she would slow down the rest of the herd as well, allowing the stragglers to catch up.

The young elephant ran to catch up with the rest! He immediately found several of his friends and began to play and visit with them. When the herd is on the move, it is more difficult to play with friends, and the young don't like the pressure of being on the move. It was only after greeting each of his friends and playing for several precious moments, that he remembered his assigned task.

By the time word reached Hannah, it was too late. As she turned to tell her part of the herd that they were going to stop and wait for the others, she smelled smoke in the air! From a distance she could see the line of fire building between her and the rest of her herd.

Meanwhile, as Emma gathered her group to catch up with the others, making sure Mother and her baby were ready to travel, she sensed danger in the air. She lifted her trunk high and smelled fire! She knew that they were in the midst of the dreaded KHEDDA. So many times Hannah had led the herd away while others were being drawn into the horseshoe of fire and led toward a corral. She realized that there was no escaping. She and her followers were all surrounded by a huge wall of fire. There was only one way to run, and that would lead them directly into the corral where the elephant catchers awaited to transport them away from freedom and into the service of man. At least they would be fed. It was better than death, unless they were ill treated of course. All these thoughts ran through Emma's mind as her herd bolted and trumpeted in fright.

The time to think was over. There was no other action to take. Koonkies, the trained elephants, were beside them and the riders were shouting "Hasti! Hasti!" which was an insistent call to the elephants.

And so Emma and about one-third of Hannah's herd were chased, urged or led into the large waiting corral. Evidently, the catchers had been tracking them for some time, as the corral was all in readiness. It had been hidden in a clump of trees and a heavy wooden fence surrounded the area. The huge wooden gate was the only way in and there was no other way out. As the entire herd was chased through the opening, and into the hands of the catchers and koonkies, many of the elephants trumpeted in terror.

Some charged the fences, and mothers searched to see that their youngest were beside them. The new babies would need milk until they were about three years old. The mothers' hoped that the captors would allow the babies to stay with them. However, they had no reason to have hope that this would happen.

As the day ended, the captured elephants were secured in the heavy wooden fences of the corral and Emma was urging them to be calm as they were tied and surrounded by koonkies. Those who fought especially hard against capture, were caged within the corral in addition to being tied to a strong tree.

The catchers were laughing and congratulating themselves on their fine catch. A cage full of chickens were released into the wild in thanks to the Great Spirit for their catch. They would have plenty of the strong beasts to train and sell to serve as builders, transporters of both goods and people, and as workers for village farms.

In the midst of the celebration was the great catcher, Lyling. Not only had he taken Shamir from the herd but he had now captured many other elephants to tame and to put to work.

As the elephants were counted, the koonkies and their Mahouts moved among the herd, stroking, calming and reassuring them.. The elephants would be given adequate food and water. While Lyling was a wily and feared catcher, he was also wiser than many. He had learned that if elephants were reassured and fed and watered regularly, more of them would live and serve man. Some catchers weakened herds through depriving them of these essentials. When this happened, large numbers of the captured elephants died. At least, when Lyling was in charge, the beasts were more respectfully treated.

As the last of the herd was moved into the stockade, Hannah and the others watched from afar. There was nothing they could do now. Many of their friends and loved ones would be taken from this place and never seen again. Hannah wept as did Maru, stroking her month old calf safely standing underneath her.

Suddenly from behind a clump of trees their emerged a small figure. It was the new baby elephant born only hours before! The mother had been captured but the new calf had been left behind. No doubt the captors did not wish to feed and care for such a young one. She had been left to die in the clearing. At least she had escaped the fire.

Hannah did not waste a moment. She motioned for the herd to stand still and she ran toward the young calf. She nudged her and led her to the safety of the herd. "Do not be afraid little one. We will take care of you now that your mother is gone."

As they moved into the herd all the others gathered around.

"Poor thing!" sighed one, "She is all alone!"

Jaku, the young elephant who had delayed giving Hannah the message as to why the herd was delayed had been stunned and sickened by what he had seen. "Perhaps if I had done as I was told, all of them would be safe. I am so sorry, Hannah. I have done a terrible thing."

"What you say is true, Jaku. You should have told me immediately as Emma directed you. However, you may have also saved the rest of us from capture. Had we turned back earlier, we may also have fallen into the trap of Lyling. Sometimes, things are not as bad as they seem. Whatever the case may be, we must now go on and hope that those whom we love will be treated kindly. There is nothing else we can do." Hannah comforted Jaku and stroked his head gently. "You say this calf belongs to Borga?"

"Yes." replied Jaku.

"She is one of my daughters," sighed Hannah sadly.

55

"Then I shall care for my sister's child," announced Maru. "I have plenty of milk and she can be a sister to my little Cali. I shall name her Borga, in honor of her mother."

The herd gathered around little Borga and reassured her through joining trunks and patting and stroking her. Maru pulled the baby under her body and offered her milk.

"Don't worry, little Cali. There will be plenty for both of you. I had twins many years ago, your older brothers Jonu and Janu. They live away from this herd now but sometimes travel with your father, Simbu. When they were small. I had plenty of milk for both."

Cali joined trunks with her new little sister and welcomed her into the warmth and security of Maru's body.

And so, in the midst of the tragedy of the terrible khedda, there was one survivor to remind them of those they had lost. It was a bit of joy in the midst of their terrible sorrow, and a reminder that life must go on.

"We are tired and hungry, I know," noted Hannah. "However, we cannot stop here." We must continue our journey and put many miles between our enemies and ourselves. Take a few minutes to eat and rest, but then we must push on. There are other catchers and hunters. Their desire to capture or kill us is great and we must keep our wits about us."

"You are right, Hannah, " said a voice from behind. It was Simbu, Shamir's father. "Lyling has his share of elephants for the day, but there is another group of catchers just east and heading this way."

"Simbu, I am so glad you are safe!" Maru was immediately beside her mate. "We did not know where you were. Did you witness the khedda?"

"Indeed we did." he announced sadly. "Jonu, Jano, several other bull elephants and I were traveling at the edge of the clearing when we smelled the fire. We did not know

56

which elephants were captured, but we were afraid all of you were there."

Hannah explained why the herd had separated to Simbu and the others.

"It is very sad, " Simbu shook his head. "My friend, Kaltus says his mate was expecting a little one. I do not see her here. I assume she was captured."

"I'm afraid Borga was one of those captured," Maru confirmed his fear. "However, Kaltus, I would like to introduce you to your new daughter. She was left behind when the herd was taken. I think Borga knew what might happen and hid her in a small clearing, hoping we would find her before the tigers did. This is little Borga, named for her mother. I will nurse her along with my own daughter, Cali."

Simbu and Kaltus acknowledged their new daughters, and rejoiced that most of the herd was still safe. Hannah told them that the group was recessing only briefly before traveling on.

"We understand your concern," Simbu replied. "We will travel with you for a while and help keep watch for enemies."

Within the hour, the herd was on the move. Before the sunset, the remaining group was several miles from the place of the khedda. They shuddered as they thought of all that had happened there but pushed on looking for a new temporary home. Hannah knew it was not far to the place she remembered, a land of plenty. She hoped the ideal place would also bring them safety. However, that was never guaranteed.

A cage full of chickens were released into the wild in thanks to the Great Spirit for their catch.

8

The Search

Meela and Cheeku had listened intently as Uncle Ramsa related to them the capture of part of Hannah's herd. Cheeku was especially unhappy. After all, the elephant herd had been his family for more than three years. Those captured were like his mothers, sisters and brothers. Ramsa did not know which of the elephants were still with the herd and which were in captivity. He did know that Hannah was still leading the herd, but he could not say if Maru was with her.

"There is only one way to find out, Meela. I will have to find Hannah and see for myself."

"I will go with you, of course," Meela insisted.

"No, my dearest. This time I must say no. Our little one is due soon and I will feel much better if I know you are safe with your family." Cheeku was so concerned for her health and safety that Meela had to agree to stay.

"I will do as you say, Cheeku. Please hurry, but be very careful and return to us safely."

Ramsa agreed to see Cheeku part of the way and show him the trail.

After a few moments of fond farewells, the two of them were on the way.

Before two days had past, they were at the spot where the dreaded khedda had occurred a few weeks before. Cheeku shuddered as he viewed the now abandoned corral and saw the parched earth where the wall of fire had been.

"This is where I must leave you, Cheeku," said Ramsa. "I must get back to my family. The herd was seen heading northwest, following the river. Good luck in finding your friends. I hope Shamir's mother is safe." In a few moments Ramsa was swinging his way back home and Cheeku was left to search alone.

In the midst of all that had happened, Cheeku had almost forgotten that he and Meela had been followed out of Burma by one of Kasha's men, Machi. However, Machi was still intent upon his task, to catch the white monkey. He was the catcher Simbu had seen in the area and he was getting closer to Cheeku.

Cheeku followed the route described by Ramsa. He stayed close enough to the river to watch for the elephants, but far enough back to stay hidden. There were villages along the Ganges and Cheeku knew that his strange appearance would draw attention so he stayed a safe distance from the river.

At one point he saw a herd of elephants ahead and his hopes were awakened, but then, as he drew closer he realized that it was not Hannah's herd. He did see some familiar elephants, though. These elephants had often shared watering spots with Hannah. He decided to ask if they knew of her whereabouts.

"We have not seen Hannah, little friend," said the matriarch, recognizing Cheeku from earlier encounters.

"We did hear the terrible news that a portion of the herd was lost in the khedda. Such a terrible thing!"

"Do you know if Maru is with Hannah?" Cheeku asked.

"I'm afraid not. I did hear that a daughter of Hannah gave birth to a little one and that she was taken in the khedda, but I do not know if it was Maru."

Hope dimmed in Cheeku's heart. He knew that Maru had been expecting. He did not know when the calf was due. Time had gone so quickly. It had been more than a year since Shamir's capture. Perhaps Maru was in Lyling's hands. She would not receive such fine treatment as Shamir. A mature elephant like Maru would be put to work in the field or used to capture other elephants. Cheeku found himself greatly saddened by what might be the fate of his adopted mother."

"Do not jump to conclusions, little friend. Hannah is old and has many daughters," the matriarch reminded Cheeku.

He must not give up hope. Whatever the fate of Maru, he must find the herd and tell them that Shamir was in good health and loved and missed them all, then he must get back to his beloved Meela.

"Follow the river northwest," suggested the queen. "That is the most probable route."

The advice seemed reasonable and so Cheeku was once again on his way.

Machi was not far behind. Some of the villagers had seen the white monkey and were willing to tell of his whereabouts for a piece of silver.

Cheeku made excellent time. The forested area provided a good cover and the August rains were almost unceasing. He hoped this extremely hot, wet weather would deter the catchers in the area. The rains, extreme heat and mosquitoes were not pleasant conditions for humans but hardly slowed down the teeming plant and animal life in the rain forest along the Ganges.

61

One morning Cheeku awoke to the chirping of birds and the sun streaming through the trees. He had not seen the sun for several days. Though the humidity was so great he was not sure his fur would ever dry out, he still moved high to the top of a bamboo tree to bask for a few minutes in the sun. As he was perched high above most of the area, he could see the shimmering forest, the meandering Ganges River and, a large grassy clearing only a short distance away. There, in the clearing, was a herd of elephants, about thirty in number. His heart leapt! Leading the herd was a very large elephant who looked from this distance, very much like Hannah!

Cheeku swung quickly down into the lower reaches of the tree and headed toward the clearing. Sure enough, the matriarch was Hannah, and close beside her was Maru with two baby elephants!

There was much rejoicing throughout when Cheeku was recognized.

"Cheeku, we thought we had lost you, too. This has been a terrible time of loss for us. First it was Shamir, then a few weeks ago, a large part of our herd." Hannah was near tears as she spoke.

"I know, Hannah. One of Meela's relatives told me of your loss. I can tell you that I am very glad to see Maru. One of the matriarchs told me that a daughter of Hannah had given birth to a new baby just before the khedda. I was afraid it was Maru."

"That was my daughter, Borga," explained Hannah. "She was captured in the khedda. However, we were able to rescue her little one." Hannah laid her trunk upon the back of little Borga. "We have named her Borga in honor of her mother."

"I am rearing her as though she were my own," Maru announced. "This is my little Cali. She is only a few months older than Borga. They are already good friends."

Cheeku listened to all of the news that had occurred in the many months since he left the herd. He also shared with them news of Shamir, as he had promised. As he described his visit with Shamir at the royal stable, his elephant family hung on every word.. He also told of the terrifying journey he and Meela had through the Chin Hills.

"Is Meela the monkey who was with you the day Shamir was captured?" Maru asked.

Cheeku nodded. "Yes indeed she is. In fact, Meela and I are expecting a little one soon. She would be with me now, but I did not want her making this journey with the birth expected soon."

All rejoiced with Cheeku, their adopted relative.

"You are so loyal and brave, Cheeku," cried Maru, her eyes glistening with tears. To follow Shamir and his captors and to travel back here to let us know of his safety putting your own life in danger, it is much more than I would have asked of anyone, even a member of the family."

"Remember, Maru. I AM a member of this family. Were it not for you and the herd adopting me, I probably would not be alive today. While those of my own kind rejected me, you took me in and loved me. I owe my life to all of you. Shamir is my brother in spirit if not in the flesh. There is nothing I would not do for him."

Maru stroked the little monkey with her trunk and playfully lifted him high in the air. "You are the only one of my children I can easily toss in the air," she laughed.

Cheeku delighted in the affectionate toss and enjoyed several hours in the company of his elephant friends. He would spend the night here and then return to his beloved Meela. He was not sure what he would do after that. For the moment he was content to enjoy his friends and rest up for the journey to rejoin Meela. He hoped he would be in time for the birth of his child.

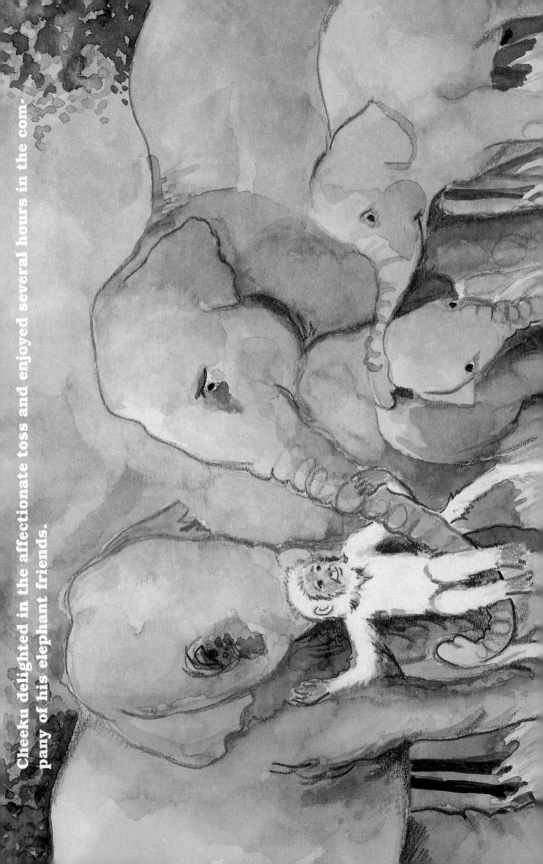

Cheeku delighted in the affectionate toss and enjoyed several hours in the company of his elephant friends.

9

The Nightmare

"Absom Tries to Help"

Shamir looked forward each day to his visit with Absom. One could not ask for a mahout kinder than this young man. While he was firm in teaching Shamir his commands, he was also friendly and affectionate. When he sensed that Shamir was especially lonely, he talked to him softly or sang to him in his clear sweet voice.

> *"Little White One, do not fear, your friend Absom is always near.*
> *While you sleep, warm breezes blow; in the morning sun, a riding we will go.*
> *The Prince and the King will keep you comfortable, free from harm.*
> *Your life is precious, you are a sacred lucky charm."*

Absom was always making up little songs to sing to Shamir. Somehow this soothed Shamir and took away some of his sadness and sorrow.

Other times, Shamir daydreamed about life in the forest. He remembered the days he wandered with Cheeku on his back. He remembered the cool waters of the Ganges when the weather was so hot; the cool mud packs and the showering of each other by he and his friends. These memories would crowd in sometimes as he napped in the afternoon.

One night Shamir dreamed of Cheeku. He saw him swinging through the forest alone. He heard him cry as his leg caught in one of the ropes Lyling had prepared for the trap. Cheeku was crying out for him to come and rescue him, but Shamir could not move. He heard the cries but could not answer them. Shamir felt himself pulling, trying to run to Cheeku. He heard the laughter of Lyling as he went to the trap and pulled the monkey from the rope and placed him in a cage. Cheeku screeched and shook the cage but it was no use. Shamir tried to chase the catcher carrying the cage but it was no use. Cheeku was looking back at him sorrowfully.

Shamir awakened from his dream moaning and covered with sweat. One of the guards was beside him, stroking him gently and drying his back with a soft cloth.

"There now, White One, do not fret. Everything will be all right." He turned to another of the guards. "Go and awaken Absom. I think White One is ill. He is moaning and almost kicked down his stall. His body is covered with sweat. I fear for his life."

Within a few minutes Absom was at Shamir's side.

"Do not cry, my friend. Nothing could be as bad as all that. You are safe. All is well. No harm will come to you. I will protect you with my life." Absom spoke softly, hummed, then sang to Shamir.

"Beautiful White One, child of the River. I will help you. Do not shiver."

It was only a bad dream. All is well. You are safe with Absom, Your fears I will quell."

While the song helped somewhat, Shamir's spirit was in turmoil. Somehow, he felt his friend Cheeku was in grave danger and there was nothing he could do about it. He simply could not stop crying and sleep would not come.

When daylight finally came, Absom was asleep beside him and the guards were asleep as well. Shamir had kept them all up most of the night with his actions. They were all exhausted, and so was Shamir. Sleep still eluded him, however. Each time he closed his eyes, the vision of Cheeku dangling from the rope and crying out to him returned.

At last, after two days and nights without sleep. Shamir finally fell into a deep sleep for several hours. Absom was so concerned that he would not leave his side.

When Shamir awoke, he was in good spirits. The nightmare had been pushed aside and the beauty of the morning warmed him and brought new energy and happiness. He looked outside and saw other animals at play and heard the birds singing. While the rainy season was not yet over, September signaled cooler weather and the rainy season would soon end. One sunny day now gave promise of many sunny days in the future. For right now, Shamir was happy and ready to go outside and enjoy the day.

Absom read the thoughts of the white elephant and perked up himself. "You seem much better, White One. Would you like to go for a ride in the sunshine? Of course you would. I can see it in your eyes. Give me a few minutes to freshen up and we will be on our way."

67

Absom had been in the same clothes for three days and nights. He had been sleeping in the stable with Shamir and smelled of elephant himself. He instructed the guards to bathe the elephant and have him ready to go for a ride in an hour. He then went home to change.

"Absom," said his mother, "Is the White One all right? We were all very worried. You smell even more like an elephant than you usually do."

"Caring for the White One is my job," said Absom proudly. "I do not mind if I smell like him. However, he is being cleaned up and I have come to clean up as well."

The wooden buckets around the house were all full from the monsoon season. Absom bathed in the refreshing waters, donned clean clothes, had a bite of lunch then made his way back to the stable. His spirits were high because his charge seemed well and happy. He knew the king would be very unhappy with him if anything were to happen to White One, which is what everyone called Shamir.

Absom whistled as he made his way back to the stable. "White One is well and we will celebrate. We will ride in the sunshine, out into the meadow. Perhaps we will go to the palace and see if Prince Risha wishes to go with us." There was a spring in his step as he made his way to Shamir's stall. He wondered why the elephant had been so unhappy, but, for now at least, everything seemed to be all right.

Shamir was clean, refreshed and trumpeted with glee when he Absom returned. He knew his friend was going to take him away from the dark stable and into the bright sunshine. He was certainly ready.

The guard who usually accompanied Absom when he rode Shamir was late. Absom saw that the elephant was impatient. "Can't we go on ahead, and let him catch up with us?" asked Absom. White One is very anxious to go."

"I don't think you should go alone. Usually you have at least three guards with you. There was a brief pause then an unusual offer. "I suppose I could accompany you myself," he suggested.

"Oh thank you! I am so anxious to take White One. I would very much appreciate it. It is only a short ride to the palace. I want to see if the prince would like to ride with us. He has many guards. I'm sure some of them can accompany us." Absom thought himself quite persuasive when his request was granted so easily.

Off went Absom riding Shamir accompanied by the guard riding his koonkie. The small party headed toward the palace, following a narrow pathway used only by the king and his servants. This was not the main road. There were too many people there. The king and his family enjoyed at least a certain amount of privacy on the palace grounds. Absom could ride all around these grounds and exercise White One. It would not be necessary nor would it be wise to leave. It was important that the white elephant be carefully guarded at all times. After all, he was more precious than gold.

"Are you enjoying being a guard for the royal white elephant, Kreeto?" Absom asked the guard as they rode. You do seem to know a great deal about elephants." Absom made conversation with the guard.

This guard had only been a royal palace guard for a few short months. Kreeto had been impressive when his skills in caring for elephants were tested. He told the king's assistant that he had grown up with elephants and would consider it a great honor to guard the white one. His credentials were impeccable and he came highly recommended. Thus far, Absom had nothing but high praise for Kreeto. He was most grateful for his presence now.

"I am enjoying this work very much. Guarding the white elephant is a sacred responsibility."

What Absom did not know was that Kreeto knew about elephants because he had worked with Kasha, elephant catcher of Akbar, ruler of the Mogul Kingdom. Credentials could be bought for a price, and guarding the elephant was a sacred responsibility - for the ruler, Akbar of India!

One night Shamir dreamed of Cheeku. He saw him swinging through the forest alone. . . . Cheeku was crying out for him to come and rescue him, but Shamir could not move.

10

Kasha's Good Fortune

"A Surprise Meeting"

As Cheeku started back southeast toward the home of Meela's family, his heart was a bit lighter. He had carried out the wishes of his friend, Shamir. While much of the family was now in captivity, he had seen Maru and Hannah. They were both well and were on their way to a place where food and water were plentiful. Life in the forest was never easy, but at least signs were hopeful that the rest of the herd would survive.

Cheeku was also aware that there had been several hunters spotted in the area. He hoped that Machi had given up stalking him, but he had no way of knowing if this was true. The heavy rains in the area would most certainly have slowed down any catchers. Besides, Lyling's party already had a large number of elephants to train and sell. Surely they were too busy to think about one small white monkey.

His hopes were true about Lyling, but not about Machi. Machi was as determined as his master, Kasha. The catcher's assistant had followed Cheeku, losing his trail when he was on the move, but picking it up again when Cheeku stopped for several hours. In fact, Machi had watched from a distance as Cheeku said his strange good-byes to his elephant family. He was astonished as he watched Maru toss the white monkey into the air. There was obviously great affection for one another. Machi only had to follow the monkey closely now and find a way to trap him before he lost his trail again. However, he must be out of sight, sound and smell of the elephant herd. His two elephants and two people would be no match for them.

Cheeku traveled quickly, swinging from tree to tree, not because he was thinking about the catchers, but because he wanted to return to Meela as rapidly as possible. Unfortunately, when one is preoccupied and focused on one area, the guard may go down on another. This is why Cheeku did not see the snare ahead. Hidden in a bunch of the tasty berries he would stop to munch on, he did not detect the noose until his arm was jerked, the noose tightened, and he was painfully suspended several feet in the air. He shrieked in both pain and fear, but the only one within earshot was not a friend, but an enemy.

"Well, well," chuckled Machi, "This looks like the work of Lyling. Just as I was trying to figure out how to capture you, you practically fall into my hands. You will be a great prize indeed for Kasha and for our king. Akbar is much amused by monkeys in the court and a white one will be especially welcomed."

Poor Cheeku had no choice but to watch as Machi held him tightly and his servant cut the rope that held him. Tears welled in Cheeku's eyes as he thought of Meela, anxiously awaiting his return. There was little chance that he would ever see his beloved again.

A cage had been prepared previously and this became the home of Cheeku for the next several weeks as he began the journey to the throne of Akbar.

As Machi was carrying his prize to Akbar, things were also changing for Shamir. As Shamir carried his Mahout, Absom, in the company of a trusted guard of the royal elephants, a plot to capture the white elephant was about to unfold.

Absom had suggested that they go to find Prince Risha to see if he would like to ride with them on this lovely sunny day. However, before they had traveled even halfway to the palace, another guard, riding another elephant, hurried up beside them.

"The prince wishes to meet the young Mahout and White One at the far edge of the palace grounds. He sent me to find you and escort you there," the guard announced most officially.

"That is strange," remarked Absom. "The prince and I never go to the far edge of the palace grounds with White One. It is too close to the edge of the forest. The king has thought it much too dangerous for us to travel there. Perhaps we should go to the palace first and check with the king."

"King Burengnong is away from the palace. I believe he is on his way to Siam. My orders are directly from the prince." The guard was insistent.

"We had better do as he says," warned Kreeto, the royal elephant guard. "It would not be wise to displease the young prince."

And so, instead of traveling to the palace where they would be surrounded by people, Absom and Shamir were traveling to the edge of the palace grounds. If anyone noticed, they did not express concern. After all, there were two palace guards with the small party.

They did not suspect that Kreeto was a traitor and the other guard was Kasha, dressed in a stolen guard's uniform. The uniform had been taken from the royal guard who usually accompanied Absom whenever he rode the white elephant. The real guard was gagged and tied in the stable, locked in a storage room which was seldom used. It would be hours before he was found.

As the party reached the edge of the palace grounds, Prince Risha was nowhere in sight. Absom's heart was pounding and he was growing very anxious. He was fearful but did not know what he might do. One guard was very close on one side. The other guard rode closely on the other side.

Kasha spoke softly put firmly. "Do not be afraid, Absom. You will not be harmed so long as you cooperate. In fact, you will continue to be mahout to the white elephant, so long as you follow our instructions completely. We will now leave the palace grounds and move into the forest. We will travel through the forest until we reach the waters of the Irrawaddy. After nightfall, we will then continue our journey to the throne of the Mogul ruler, Akbar."

Absom feared for his life but he was also very attached to the white elephant. He decided that his only hope now was to do as the captors said. He had been reared with the prince and knew several of the languages spoken in these areas. That is how he had helped Lyling take the white elephant out of Bengal country into Burma. He was not sure what would happen, but he decided to remain quiet and do as he was told. His oath to his king was to protect the white elephant. Whatever the future might bring, he must try to do that.

The small party then escaped into the forest and traveled several miles before stopping. When they did stop, Kasha and Kreeto rubbed dirt onto the head and legs and onto the body of Shamir. They covered him with ragged blankets and did the same to their own elephants. The guard uniforms were packed away and the two men donned the clothing of peasants. They also instructed Absom to don peasant clothing. As night fell, they were at the bank of the Irrawaddy. A large river barge awaited the party. The three elephants, two men and the boy boarded the barge and moved southward toward the Bay of Bengal. The barge moved quietly through the waters, now calm but greatly swollen from the continual rains. No one noticed as they traveled throughout the night. By the morning, they were far from the palace and heading toward the Gulf of Martaban. It started to rain again, but the party did not stop until they reached the mouth of the river. There they boarded a large sea vessel, *THE MOGUL STAR*. The three elephants were taken below into the bowels of the ship. Absom was also taken below, but either Kasha or Kreeto remained with him at all times. It would not really have mattered whether they did or not though. Absom soon discovered that the ship was filled with servants and guards of Akbar. There would be no escaping from his captors.

The ship traveled north out of the waters of the Gulf of Martaban and into the Bay of Bengal, traveling several miles out from the mainland, but following the coastline.

As they sailed, the rains continued to fall, sometimes pounding fiercely against the large sea craft. Absom was often ill, seasick from the constant beating of the waves and thrashing of the ship.

In a few days, the ocean seemed calm and the ship moved into port. Through a port hole, Absom recognized the city of Chittagong. Here the ship took on fresh supplies and a few other passengers. Absom was surprised to see a man carrying a caged white monkey coming aboard. The stranger waved to another man who stood at the shore holding on to two large elephants.

"Very strange," thought Absom. "I have never seen a white monkey before. I wonder where he came from."

As the ship left port, Absom watched the man carrying the monkey move down to the area where he and Kasha sat with Shamir.

"So we were both successful," laughed Machi. "I captured the white monkey and you captured the white elephant. King Akbar will be very pleased with us."

Shamir could not believe his eyes. There, not six feet away from him, was his friend, Cheeku, caged and frightened but at least he was alive!

Kasha spoke softly but firmly. "Do not be afraid, Absom. You will not be harmed so long as you cooperate."

11

THE MOGUL STAR

At first Cheeku did not recognize his friend, Shamir. The dirt rubbed into his skin and the ragged blankets disguised his color. It was only when the elephant trumpeted that he looked closely and recognized him. Cheeku greeted him warmly but the others did not know what was being said as they did not speak the language of the jungle.

"I think these two may know each other," observed Kasha, "Remember, I saw the white monkey leaving the royal stable the night I sent you after him, Machi."

"They do seem to be glad to see each other. Perhaps they are not just dumb animals after all,"
added Machi.

Absom said nothing but he was acutely aware of the strong communication between the two. When Kasha and Machi went upstairs together that night, he was glad that they invited Kreeto to go along with them. This gave him the opportunity to move the cage close to the stall where Shamir was both caged and tied.

The two seemed delighted to see each other. Shamir's trunk reached through the cage and stroked the monkey. "Cheeku, how in the world did you get here. I never expected to see you again."

"I could say the same for you, Shamir. You were at the royal stable of King Burengnong the last time I saw you. I see your mahout is also with you," Cheeku motioned toward Absom.

The two friends chattered away, telling each other of the adventures they had both had since last they met. Cheeku shared the joy of his mate, Meela, expecting a little one and the sadness of not being there with her for the birth. He also told Shamir of the khedda and how many members of his family were now in the hands of Lyling. Shamir was relieved to know of the safety of his mother and the birth of little Cali and rescue of baby Borga, but very upset they so many of his sisters and aunts were now in captivity.

"I will say, though, Lyling was never unkind to me," admitted Shamir. He seems to treat his elephants with respect. He did see that Absom became my mahout, which has been the real bright spot in my capture. Absom is kind and wonderful to me. He has taught me many valuable lessons and sings to me when I am sad. Next to you, Cheeku, he is the best friend I ever had. When Kasha captured me, he brought Absom as well. I am sorry for his family, but I feel much better knowing he is with me."

As the two friends talked together, Absom watched and listened. He did not know exactly what they were saying but he did have a strong bond with animals and he knew at

82

some point they were speaking of him. "These two are good friends," he concluded, "They speak together the way Prince Risha and I do. They laugh and cry together. If they must be captives, it is good that they can be together.

So intent upon observing the two friends, Absom had not noticed that the winds had picked up again. The rain began to come down in sheets and the strong ship was being knocked about as though it were a small toy. A huge crash of thunder brought Absom and the animal friends to the realization that they were in the midst of a terrible storm. The thrashing of *THE MOGUL STAR* was continuous and frightening. Huge waves picked up the ship and threw it down again cruelly. Absom found himself being thrown from one side of the ship to the other. Water spewed through the hold of the ship, spraying all the cargo stored there. As Absom was tossed back next to Shamir, he grabbed hold of the elephant with one hand and held tightly to Cheeku's cage with the other. He saw Kasha and Machi starting down the stairs, crying out to them. However, their cries were lost when one huge bolt of lightning struck the bow of the ship. The winds of the typhoon picked up ship with such force that it broke in half as it hit the water again. The contents of the ship were now spread throughout at least a square mile of the sea.

Absom still held tightly to both Shamir and Cheeku. However, he soon realized that Shamir was firmly tied to a huge iron weight. If he did not free him from the weight, he would surely drown.

First, Absom opened the cage that held Cheeku, whereupon Cheeku jumped on Shamir's back and hugged him tightly about the neck. Secondly, Absom removed the small knife he carried from its sheath and began to saw through the thick rope. The wet rope was much too swollen to attempt to untie. At last he cut through enough that Shamir could pull away from the weakened grip. As

Absom completed this task, the last few seconds working underwater, the entire ship was enveloped in water and was sinking fast. Absom swam toward Shamir and tried to mount him. However at that moment, a large board from Shamir's stall fell and struck Absom on the head rendering him unconscious. His body began to sink. Within seconds, Cheeku swam underwater and pulled the boy within Shamir's reach. Together they pulled him onto Shamir's back using the strength of Shamir and the dexterity of Cheeku to accomplish the task. Cheeku held the boy's head above water and directed Shamir to swim toward the beam of light which identified the shore. Fortunately, the ship had been following the shoreline when the storm struck. They had been blown about ten miles out to sea, but Shamir was strong and determined. Using his trunk as a snorkel, the strong, young elephant guided by the monkey holding tightly to the boy, moved rapidly through the water. The storm had happened in early evening so most of their journey was made in the darkness. The sea was still churning when their journey began but had calmed considerably when they reached the shore several hours later, shortly before dawn.

The three friends were a few miles north of Chittagong, at the eastern mouth of the Ganges. There were a few huts within view but the world was still sleeping.

"Shamir," whispered Cheeku, "I know the way back to our herd from here. Machi brought me this way before we boarded the ship."

Shamir was exhausted from the long swim but was delighted to hear that Cheeku could lead them home. He looked at Absom, still unconscious, but breathing evenly. "Before we leave, we must make sure Absom is all right."

There was a small hut not far from the shore. As dawn was breaking, Shamir carried Absom to the small porch and laid him gently beside the doorway. Through the window, they could see a sleeping couple and a small child. Confident that Absom would be found and cared for, Cheeku and Shamir hurried away while most of the world still slept, disappearing into the forest beside the Ganges.

Using his trunk as a snorkel, the strong young elephant, guided by the monkey holding tightly to the boy, moved rapidly through the water.

12

The Homecoming

Even after his exhausting swim, Shamir was exhilarated and anxious to return home. Cheeku was even more excited, knowing that by now he would be a father. Meela would also be very worried since he had been gone much longer that expected. Perhaps news of his capture had reached her, or perhaps she feared for his life. There are many dangers for monkeys in the rain forest.

Shamir and Cheeku traveled day and night, stopping only long enough to rest and eat. By now, the days were getting shorter and a bit cooler after the extremely hot, wet summer. While they traveled quickly, they also traveled carefully. Neither wished to find himself in the hands of hunters. They were both weary of being royal pawns and ready for the freedom and the forest and the warmth and love of family and friends.

After several days they reached the place where Cheeku had said good-bye to Meela many weeks ago. It was late afternoon and the forest was relatively quiet as many creatures napped. Cheeku swung off of Shamir's back and high into the trees, seeking his young family. While Meela was nowhere to be seen, her uncle, Ramsa, rested nearby.

"Cheeku!" He exclaimed, "How good to see you. We were all very worried when you did not show up within a few days."

"It is good to see you, too, Ramsa, but most of all I hunger to see Meela and our little one," responded Cheeku rather impatiently.

"You will have to wait a bit longer, I am afraid," sighed Ramsa. "Meela was so concerned about you that she left a few days ago to find your elephant family. I went with her as far as I could, but I had to come back and care for my family. Meela's aunt is quite ill."

"I am sorry to hear that, Ramsa. I had hoped Meela would stay right here in the safety of her family. I told her of my concern." Cheeku was a bit frustrated that his beloved was not there.

"She did follow your instructions, Cheeku. She waited until the birth of your son before she left.," Ramsa reminded Cheeku.

"A son! I have a son. Did you hear that, Shamir." Cheeku was ecstatic. He jumped on Shamir's back, turned around several times as in a dizzying dance then swung through the trees in rapid motion before settling back beside Ramsa.

Cheeku had not cared whether the baby was a girl or boy. Either would have received the same response. The reality of the birth was what brought him such great joy. Now, he was more anxious that ever to be united with his growing family.

"Meela waited until she had her full strength back, then decided that her place was with you. If you had run into some sort of trouble, she thought she might be able to help. You know how strong-minded she is," Ramsa shook his head in mock frustration.

"Indeed I do," laughed Cheeku, "That is one of the reasons I love her so much, and also why I will never understand her."

Ramsa wished the friends well and the two of them set off immediately to find Meela, the baby and Shamir's family. It was beginning to look like this might happen at the same time.

Again they traveled both day and night taking only rest and nourishment when necessary. Within a few day, they were in the area where Cheeku had been captured. They had passed the place where the dreaded khedda had taken place. The corral was now abandoned but remnants of ropes, broken cages and burning brush were all about. Shamir had shuddered when he thought of what had taken place here. He wondered where Emma and the rest of his captured family were now. He hoped they had mahouts as kind as Absom had always been to him. He took some comfort in the fact they Lyling did seem to have respect for elephants and saw to it that those in his charge were well cared for. Never mind that it was because he expected to get more work out of the beasts this way rather than for love of them. Nevertheless, it was the truth according to Sheba, and Lena, the elephants who had assisted in Shamir's capture.

After showing Shamir the place where he had been captured by Kasha, in the trap set by Lyling, the two friends moved on toward the area where Hannah and the remaining herd had last been seen. Hopefully, Meela had followed the same path.

89

Absom awakened to the smell of rice and bananas, simmering on the stove. He had a terrible headache and had no idea where he was or how he got there.

A young girl, who appeared to be about seven years old, was standing beside him. "Mama, Mama, the boy wakes up! she scurried to get her mother who was across the room preparing lunch.

"So, the sleeping one finally awakens, " she said softly, her lilting voice sounding almost musical. I told my husband you would be waking up soon. He was about ready to give up."

"How long have I been asleep? Who are you? Where am I? How did I get here?" Absom was anxious to clear his muddled brain.

"One question at a time," the woman laughed. "You have been sleeping about three weeks in our home. Since you were asleep when you were found on our porch, I am not exactly sure how much longer. The woman with healing power was here a few days ago and said you had evidently received a severe blow to the head. There was nothing to do but let you sleep and pray that Allah would heal you. You are in a small sea village, south of Chittagong. As to how you got here, that is quite a mystery. The ship, *THE MOGUL STAR*, was wrecked in a storm the night before we found you. If you were on that ship, you are the only known survivor. Word is that all else was lost. King Akbar was most upset since it carried much valuable cargo and some of his most trusted servants. Were you on the ship?" the woman paused to inquire.

"Yes," answered Absom, the events of the moments before the storm struck were beginning to return to his mind.

"As to who I am, my name is Jahlona. This is my daughter Cita, and my husband, Moglee, is out fishing." The woman hugged Cita to her, and they laughed softly together. They seemed happy and relieved that their unknown patient was finally awake. "We were all very worried about you," Jahlona added, "and, incidentally, we would very much like to know the name of the boy who has slept in our midst for so many days.

"I am Absom," from the kingdom of Burma. "I was a captive on that ship."

"Why would anyone want to capture a young boy?" asked Jahlona, astonished at his words.

"Because I was mahout to the young white elephant he was also capturing," answered Absom.

Absom then told them all he could remember of those hours on the ship. He told how he had tried to free White One as the ship was falling apart. "I don't suppose you saw a white elephant about?" he asked half jokingly.

"No, but that does not mean he was not here. Can elephants swim?" she asked.

"They are excellent swimmers," Absom assured her.

"Perhaps you rescued the elephant then he rescued you, or perhaps you floated in on a piece of wood and landed on my porch. Think what you will, somehow, you alone were spared from drowning in the fierce sea. Allah be praised!" She rejoiced.

Absom thought, "Perhaps there was a white elephant and a small monkey, too." However, Absom did not speak these words. If the elephant was alive, he did not want the others to know.

"There was a large piece of the boat underneath me. The waves could have swept me in here and carried the wood out again," Absom offered this explanation.

"I see, Absom. That is what you would like us to believe," laughed Johlana. "I understand."

Absom liked this woman very much. She could read the things in his heart as well as the words he said.

91

"No doubt there is no use looking for a white elephant. No doubt you were unable to release him from the heavy weight and he died in the shipwreck with all the others," there was mock seriousness in her voice.

"Thank you for your understanding, Johlana," Absom's eyes glistened with tears as he spoke. Within his mind there was a dim picture of White One, with the help of the monkey, lifting him and carrying him to safety. He somehow knew that he had been rescued from certain death by White One and the monkey. He had visions of them traveling, as he slept, through the rain forest and home to their loved ones. There was nothing he would do to jeopardize their safety.

"I must begin my journey home, back to Toungoo, as soon as I can travel, " said Absom resolutely. My family will be very worried."

"Had I a boy as kind and wonderful as you. I would want him back as soon as possible," sympathized Johlana. "My husband has a strong boat. The seas are calmer now. I am sure he will take you home."

"But, that will take many days! I could walk." Absom suggested.

"The angel who laid you on our steps expected us to see that you were returned home safely," Johlana insisted, adding a mischievous wink. "My husband will take you, and that is that."

Absom believed that if Johlana insisted, it would happen.

"Cita moved closer to Absom and asked, "Are you hungry? Mother has prepared a delicious lunch. We need to fatten you up a bit. Each day my mother held you up while I filled your mouth with warm broth. Little of it stayed in, I'm afraid, but it was enough to keep you from starving."

Absom looked from lovely mother to beautiful child. How fortunate he was to be placed on the steps of such loving people. His friend had chosen well.

When Moglee returned to the hut, he was elated to see the patient alive and well.

"You will finally have your bed back, Cita," he joked.

Cita blushed. "I did not mind giving up my sleeping mat to Absom."

The next few days were filled with walks along the beach, eating wholesome food, and laughing and talking with his new friends. He even made up a song about Cita.

"Cita of the laughing eyes, how beautiful is your smile,
Image of your mother, sweet Johlana, such a happy, gifted child."

A few days later, as he and Moglee started on their journey to Toungoo. Johlana and Cita helped them load the food and water they would need.

"We will miss you, dear Absom, " Johlana cried softly. Your music and your gentle spirit have brought joy to our house."

"Indeed, " Cita agreed shyly. "It will not be the same without you."

"I will miss your family very much. You have sacrificed much for my safely. Somehow I will find a way to reward you for your kindness to me." Absom found his eyes also welling up with tears as he hugged each of them.

"We must go, Absom," reminded Moglee, "The sun rises higher in the sky and we have a long day ahead."

As the small fishing boat left the shore the friends waved until they were no longer visible to each other.

After several days, Absom and Moglee arrived in Toungoo. When Absom walked to the door of his home, he was no longer a boy, but had grown into a young man. At first his mother did not recognize him. When she did, she wept tears of great joy. All had thought him lost.

The guard who had been tied up in the stable storage room had guessed what had happened. A woodsman had seen the party changing into peasant clothes and boarding the ship. He had also identified the catcher, Kasha, as heading the party. When *THE MOGUL STAR* was sunk, they were all saddened for they knew that Absom and White One had been carried on board.

Prince Risha was happy to see his friend again, though the king was sorry to lose his prize white elephant. They all marveled at his miraculous escape, and profusely thanked Moglee for bringing Absom home. His small boat was filled with gifts and gold coins for caring for this very special young man.

Meanwhile, back in the rain forest, Shamir and Cheeku grew more excited as they reached the area where Hannah had been seen only a few days before. Cheeku had climbed a tree so that he might look down on the clearing.

"I see them, and Meela is with them, too," he said excitedly. "But it is strange. Hannah is lying down and the herd is gathered around her."

Shamir's heart was filled with anguish for he thought he knew what this meant.

"Hurry, Cheeku," he urged, "There isn't a moment to lose."

"My name is Jahjona. This is my daughter, Cita. We were all very worried about you."

13

The Death of Hannah

The homecoming was a mixture of sadness and happiness. Cheeku greeted his mate, Meela and his baby son with warmth and affection, but it was not the time for an open display of joy. Maru joined her trunk with Shamir's and let him know that she was relieved and happy to see him, but she then led him immediately to Hannah.

"Hannah," she whispered, "Shamir is here. He escaped from his captors. Little Cheeku is here as well."

"Good," rasped Hannah weakly, "It will be possible to bid them farewell."

Shamir and Cheeku moved into the inner circle where the family had gathered to say their good-byes. Everyone knew that it was Hannah's time but still, it was very difficult to lose someone so wise, so wonderful, and so very dear to them all. Hannah had been the queen for at least ten years.

When her older sister had died the leadership of the herd had fallen to her. While Hannah had been a superb leader, there were also some dark memories of perceived failures. The khedda, which took many of their group, was the most recent of these. Hannah had never stopped grieving over that event, though she had gone bravely on. There was also the capture of Shamir which had caused her great pain. However, here was her beautiful grandson, back again.

"Dearest Grandmother," sobbed Shamir, "Do you really have to leave us. I was so looking forward to our long talks. You always knew the right answer. You always loved me even when I made a mistake. So many times, you were there to help me and anyone else who was in trouble. You taught me how to love others, to be a good friend, and the value of working together. You also encouraged me to be proud of who I was, no matter what others thought. Dear Hannah, what will we do without you?"

The old matriarch raised her head a bit and made it known that she was about to speak. The forest was still as even the birds and other creatures seemed to know that the words about to be spoken would be carved in their memories forever.

"My dearest family, you will get by just fine without me, In fact, you will move faster through the forest. These past few months as my last set of teeth has worn down, chewing has been very difficult and many times you have had to wait for me. I want you all to know, though, that I love each and every one of you. Each of you have offered special gifts to our herd, and have made living with you a pleasure."

Hannah pulled herself up slowly and painfully in order to look into the eyes of each member of the herd. She then addressed each of them, reaching out weakly to touch trunks as she spoke. "Lannie, you were always able to calculate and measure, somehow enabling you to tell me how long the food supply would last. Your methodical

97

reasoning saved this herd from starving on more than one occasion." Lannie stared shyly at the ground, honored by his queen.

Hannah then turned to Jaku, who had lingered, cavorting and playing with friends instead of delivering the message from his mother, Emma, on the day of the khedda. "Jaku, you are so like your mother, Emma. You see what others do not: the beauty of the raindrops, the pink and orange in the sunset, and the blue of the waters are all richer because you helped us see the forest with wider vision. You are also very honest, shouldering responsibility rather than shirking it. I am proud of the way you have matured these past months."

Hannah then reached out to Simbu, Shamir's father. While he lived away from the herd as was the practice of adult male elephants, he was also available when needed, and was an important member of the family. Hannah had great respect for him. "Simbu, you are the strongest and mightiest of all of us. Somehow when you are among us, any task seems possible. You also seem to know just when you will be needed and have been right here at my side. Had it not been for your strength, Simbu, we could never have pulled Shamir from the pit."

All the herd nodded in agreement remembering the incident that happened several years ago.

Hannah continued her final words as she caught sight of Kisha, one of the younger female elephants who was the group musician. "Dear Kisha, how I will miss your sweet songs. When we tramped through the forest, your voice brought us a rhythm and a beat to move by. Whatever the season, there was always music to say what words could not. There was singing to accentuate our joy when hearts were glad, and soothing songs to comfort us when our spirits were overcome with sadness." As Hannah finished these words, a tear trickled from the eye of Kisha, spilling onto Hannah's trunk as she offered a farewell grasp.

Hannah now addressed Maru who stood close by, deeply moved by her mother's words and also wondering what would happen next. Hannah grasped her trunk and began, "My lovely daughter, Maru, you were always the great peace maker and negotiator. When we quarreled with each other, you seemed to be able to bring us together again. You taught us to think of others and not merely of ourselves. You have been my right hand helper for many years."

Maru wept when her mother spoke and felt the impending tremendous loss deep in her heart.

Hannah next turned to the great orator of the herd. A large, handsome bull, he always had the right words on his lips. "Talman, you were always our great spokesman. You always knew just what to say in expressing our grief, our happiness, or frustration. There were times when your words lifted me from the deepest despair."

"Thank you, my Queen. Your very presence has always been of great inspiration," Talman acknowledged her words to him.

Hannah then noticed Delpha, a shy one who seemed to be hanging back. "Come forward, Delpha, I want to be sure you know how important you are and how much you have meant to me." Hannah joined trunks with Delpha and spoke encouragingly, "You were the quiet and reflective one. Some of us would let the perils of the day crowd out a time to think and re-focus, but not you. You have saved us many mistakes by taking time to think. I have always valued your counsel."

As when Hannah spoke to each, the herd acknowledged the truth of Hannah's words.

The noble matriarch spoke to each member of the herd, thanking them for their contribution to the welfare of the herd. No matter how large or small, she remembered each of them. Her voice seemed a bit stronger as you joined trunks with Shamir then stroked little Cheeku.

"You two are very special. Your friendship has been a model for us all. The sacrifices you were willing to make for each other serves as a model of friendship to all of us. When others rejected you, you found each other. When those who had rejected you begged forgiveness, you gave it."

Hannah coughed and laid her head down, struggling now for breath.

"A few months ago, my younger sister, Emma, would have been your queen. She was the next in age and very wise indeed. However, Emma, and most of our other older sisters and cousins were lost in the khedda. Therefore, that leaves Maru the next in line. I know you are a little young to be queen, Maru, but you are very wise and the herd will listen to you. Lead with firmness and wisdom for the position of matriarch is a sacred trust. The safety of our family lies in your hands. Whenever a mistake is made by someone, learn from it, but move on, for dwelling on problems will not bring solutions. Discipline in love and live in peace. And now, I must leave you. Farewell my dear family."

Hannah moaned once more then fell back, her mighty head thumping gently in the soft grass. Her body was motionless and the forest was quiet as all paid homage to their wise queen who was now departed.

The elephants all stood around her body for several hours. They would stroke her, nudge her and cry. Somehow it was hard to realize that she was gone.

At last Maru lifted her head and spoke, "It is time to move on. Hannah was leading us to a place where food is plentiful and we are far away from the humans who would capture us. She has told me the way to go, and we must

100

leave soon. Her body will feed the forest she loved and she will be a part of it forever. Now we must eat and get ready to travel."

The herd nodded and followed Maru's instructions. They all knew that she was right. No matter how deep their grief, life must go on and they must continue on the journey they had begun. They would now trust Maru to lead them just as they had trusted Hannah for so many years.

By first light, they were on their way. Shamir, Cheeku, Meela and their infant had joined the travelers.

The noble matriarch spoke to each member of the herd, thanking them for their contribution to the welfare of the herd.

14

Visit From an Old Friend

Twelve years had past since the death of Hannah. Maru had made an excellent leader for the herd just as her mother had predicted. The group had found a place deep in the rain forest, far away from the prying eyes of elephant catchers and hunters, who were seeking either laborers or ivory tusks. While the elephant family still had to move often to find feeding grounds, the vegetation was so lush and the new growth came so quickly, that a circle could be made from season to season as new vegetation replaced that which had been used up by the elephants and other creatures who lived in the forest.

Meela and Cheeku still lived close by, though they were no longer young. As Shamir reached full adulthood, Meela and Cheeku reached maturity. However, they had several offspring surrounding them, and it was a happy, ever-growing family. The baby monkey, born shortly before the death of Hannah, was unusual but quite beautiful. He had much white over his body, like his father, Cheeku. However, he was also splotched generously with the brown of the other monkeys in the family. He lived close by with his mate and several siblings.

Shamir now lived on the edge of the herd, often traveling with his father and brothers but sometimes traveling alone. One day, when Shamir was by himself, he had an experience that caused him great fear, then confusion, and finally relief. This moment in his life would be forever etched in his mind.

Absom was now the King's elephant keeper in Burma. His love for the creatures in his charge was well known and had won him accolades from far and near. It was said that Absom could get more work from the elephants in his charge than anyone in Burma or any kingdom. This is because the elephants knew that Absom would feed them well, give them the necessary rest, and allow them time to be together. He knew that elephants were very social creatures and would thrive in the company of one another. He also knew that when kept apart, his charges were unhappy, very likely to produce less, and live shorter lives.

Of course, King Burengnong still missed the beautiful white elephant captured by Kasha then lost in the shipwreck that almost cost Absom his life. "Ah, if only he had been able to save the white elephant!" he would often muse with his son, Prince Risha.

Absom had never shared with a living soul his suspicion that the white elephant had first saved him and then run for freedom. In fact, he knew of no other way his rescue was possible. His last thoughts before he awakened in the house of Moglee and Johlana were in cutting the heavy rope holding White One to the iron weight.

One happy result of his rescue, was the formation of a lifelong friendship with the family who had cared for him during those weeks he was recovering from his injuries. In fact, his friendship with Cita, the daughter had grown into an enduring love. Recently, he had taken Cita to be his wife and he was happier than he had ever been.

For their honeymoon trip, the king had given him several weeks off to travel and explore. He had decided to take his new bride for a trip into the rain forest to explore the beauty there, and to fulfill a special wish. Absom hoped to find the white elephant, not to capture him, but to confirm his belief that his friend was alive after the mysterious rescue of Absom from the shipwreck. He also hoped to find the white monkey. He remembered releasing the monkey from his cage just before he went underwater to cut the rope. He had surmised that the white monkey had assisted in his rescue. Perhaps he and White One were still together. At any rate, he had a great deal to thank those two special creatures for. Not only did he owe his life to them, but they had also placed him in the hands of the family that he had grown to love almost as his own. His lovely bride, Cita, was about to hear his story of how he thought the rescue had taken place.

As Absom went through each detail of what had happened as best he could recall, and how he thought he had then ended up on her doorstep, Cita listened intently. As he completed the tale, Cita sighed then chucked softly, "Well, I knew you didn't really think you had ridden the waves in on a piece of wood while you were totally unconscious. However, you did not seem to want us to even ask about any other alternatives."

"That is because I wanted White One to have his freedom. I knew the king would send me to look for him if he thought there was any chance he might be alive." Absom had even convinced Lyling that there was no hope for White

One. (Usually, Absom was very truthful, but he believed that expressing his hope that White One was still alive would send the catchers out to seek for him. Besides, he did not know for a fact, he only suspected.)

Lyling had not seemed as interested in searching for white elephants in his later years. He was willing to rest on the high level of achievement already reached. He had retired as chief elephant catcher only two years before, and no one had stepped forward to take his place. The old white elephant, Kordo, was still living, but was obviously on his last set of teeth. When he was gone, King Burengnong would probably begin to press again for white elephants. For now, the matter was not a matter of discussion.

And so, here were Cita and Absom, the happy newlyweds, riding through the rain forest on Absom's favorite elephant, Lena. Lena had been with Absom since he was only a boy. In fact, she had been with Lyling and Absom when Shamir had been captured. Only a little older than Shamir, she had now reached maturity. Lena was happy to be making the journey. Though she had been in captivity since she was very young, the rain forest seemed familiar and inviting. It was good to be a part of such a happy adventure. She hoped they would be successful in finding Shamir. She had been very fond of him in their time together. Not only had they crossed the Chin hills together, but she had seen him often while he was in Toungoo, living in the stable next to his.

Since Absom was mahout to both elephants, Lena had spent a great deal of time assisting in the training of the white elephant. She had taught him to sit properly, to hold his head high in the parade, and to move slowly and smoothly when he carried the young prince. While Absom had given the directions, it had been Lena who encouraged Shamir and modeled the behavior necessary to succeed in the court. She had also comforted him in those first few weeks when he was so homesick for the forest and his family.

Lena had been greatly saddened when the news of Shamir's capture by Kasha had reached her ears. She had been devastated when she heard Shamir had been lost at sea in the sinking of *THE MOGUL STAR*. In the months they had known each other, she had learned much of the rain forest, of Hannah, of Maru, and of Shamir's friend Cheeku. She had been in the stall beside Shamir, the night Cheeku had come to warn him about Kasha. That was the same night Shamir had told her about Cheeku, the white monkey, and the daring rescue from the pit. Lena had grieved for weeks as everyone in the royal stable spoke of the loss of White One.

And now, here was Absom speaking as though he suspected that Shamir might be alive! Not only might he be alive, but Shamir was probably responsible for the rescue of Absom from the wreck of *THE MOGUL STAR!* How Lena hoped these suspicions were true.

One night while Absom and Cita slept, Lena was wide awake and restless. The moon was full and the night sounds of the forest kept her awake. She looked along the Ganges River and noted how the water glistened in the moonlight. As she drank in the beauty of the forest and felt the cool breeze of the night wind in her face, a large handsome elephant came into view. At first, Lena thought she was dreaming. Perhaps it was the long day's journey, or perhaps it was something unusual she had eaten that day, fermented berries perhaps, but the elephant who appeared at the waters edge, seemed to be white!

While most mahouts would never think of sleeping with their elephant untied, Absom trusted Lena completely. She moved unfettered toward the place where she had seen the figure of the elephant. She gasped as she grew closer. He was larger, handsomer, and had a more confident manner

108

about him, but there was no mistaking the way he tossed his head and splashed water over his body. It was Shamir!

Lena moved closer. Shamir lifted his trunk sniffing the air. He knew he was in the presence of another elephant, but he was a bit confused. It was not a scent he recognized at once, yet it was strangely familiar. He scanned his memory for recognition, then heard a faintly familiar voice.

"Shamir! Shamir! Look over this way. It is Lena! Do you remember me?" She was so excited she could hardly contain her excitement. Her heart was pounding. Her joy was unbounding.

Shamir moved quickly through the water and to the place beside Lena. The two joined trunks and patted each other affectionately. The mind of each pulled them back to their happy days together and they realized how much they had missed each other.

"My dearest Lena, I cannot believe it is really you. Captivity would be a very dark chapter in my life were it not for you and Absom. How is he? Did he make it home to you? I have so worried about his safety." Tears glistened in the eyes of Shamir as he spoke of Absom.

"Absom is fine," Lena assured him, "In fact, that is why I am here."

Lena told Shamir to come with her quietly. The two friends moved to the place where Absom and his young bride slept. Shamir wept with joy as he saw that his young friend, now a grown man, lay sleeping peacefully, embraced by a beautiful young woman.

The elephants moved away so not to disturb the sleeping pair. "Not only did you give Absom his life, you also gave him the love of his life," Lena laughed softly. She then explained how Absom had lived with Moglee, Johlana, and the girl, Cita, while he recovered from the shipwreck.

"I knew they would be kind to him when I saw the young girl sleeping there," Shamir reminisced. "Cheeku and I

109

wanted to be sure he would be cared for properly. After all, had he not saved us, we could not have rescued him. Shamir described how Absom had released Cheeku, then cut the rope from the iron weight from Shamir's leg, even as the water inundated the bowels of the ship. He told Lena about the large board that had knocked Absom unconscious, and relived the tale of how Shamir and Cheeku had lifted Absom from the waters and started for the shore. "Cheeku held Absom's head above water while I swam for shore. It was a long swim but I never doubted that we would make it. The lights of the village guided us and it was as though the finger of God pointed out the fisherman's house to us."

The two friends talked through the night, spilling over with the happiness of seeing one another and sharing the joys and sorrows of the past years. Shamir told of the death of Hannah and the rising up of Maru as the new matriarch. Lena told of the retirement of Lyling, the elephant catcher, and of the many elephants who now lived in the royal stables. Of course she now knew Borga, mother of little Borga. Old Emma had died and Borga was the leader of the group in captivity. She knew Borga would be happy to hear that her little daughter had been rescued and was almost grown.

"My mother, Maru, took little Borga in and reared her as a daughter, along with my sister, Cali," explained Shamir.

As dawn broke through the darkness, Absom awakened, kissed his still sleeping wife, Cita, and stood up and stretched. He looked around for Lena and decided he had probably gone to the Ganges for a morning drink. As Absom grew close to the water, he first saw Lena drinking then he saw the large white figure beside her. There was no mistaking it! It was White One!

Absom saw Shamir at about the same time Shamir caught a glimpse of Absom. The joy at seeing one another was almost inexpressible. They laughed. They cried. Shamir picked up Absom gently and placed him on his back. Absom stroked, hugged and kissed the beautiful animal, all the time singing;

> *"White One, White One, beautiful and free!*
> *Through these many years I have wondered about thee.*
> *I know thou saved me from the depths of the sea,*
> *Hast thou also wondered and thought about me!"*

The voice was rich and deep but still beautiful and melodious. Shamir remembered how that singing had brought him through the dark days of captivity.

"Come White One, you must meet my lovely Cita. After all, you practically laid me in her arms," Absom laughed.

By this time, Cita had awakened and was watching in astonishment the frolicking of the elephant and the young man.

As they turned to come to her side, she laughed, "So this is what all the excitement is about! I must assume that this is the elephant you call "White One."

As Absom and Cita sat down for a breakfast of fresh fruit, the two elephants, too excited to eat before, now ate ravenously from some fruiting trees nearby.

"There is something I must tell you, Absom. It is about that morning we found you on our porch. I've been afraid to say anything before, not sure whether or not I was dreaming, not wishing to raise your hopes," Cita first hesitated, then began to speak urgently, the words tumbling out, having been kept inside for years. "As I slept in my room, I remember waking very early hearing unfamiliar sounds outside. I opened my eyes just a little and I thought I saw a white elephant and a white monkey staring at me through my window. You were motionless lying on the

111

back of the elephant. All of you disappeared briefly. The next thing I knew, the elephant and monkey were running toward the forest and a little later, I found you lying unconscious on the porch."

Absom stared at Cita incredulously, "Why have you said nothing to me, before."

"At first I thought it was a dream. Later, I realized that you did not want anyone to think the elephant was alive for fear they would try to capture him. It seemed best to say nothing. I was not sure it actually happened until this minute seeing the white elephant before me. All I really need to see now is a white monkey." Cita laughed and looked all around her, then shouted in astonishment "That's him! That's the monkey."

As though on cue, Cheeku chose that moment to swing through the trees looking for Shamir.

"So there you are, Shamir," said the old monkey. At first he was startled and a little frightened when he saw the two people, but since Shamir did not seem upset, he realized that these were friends, not enemies. As he looked closer at the young man, he somehow knew this was Absom. He did not even seem surprised when Shamir told him who Cita was.

That morning turned to afternoon, then afternoon to evening, then evening to nighttime. The friends played and talked and sang together. The golden memories of the past danced before them as did the happiness and pleasures of the present. For this moment, none of them thought of the future and the time of separation that would come. That night, as Absom and Cita fell into one another's arms, happy and exhausted, Lena and Shamir slipped quietly away for time alone, together. Shamir knew he loved Lena, and she also expressed her love for him.

For two days, the visit continued, then the time for good-byes came. Absom stroked his friend and sang to him once more, his eyes wet with tears.

112

"Good-bye my friend the White One, beautiful and free,
Wherever I am, I will always remember thee.
Live here in the beauty of the Forest green,
But stay carefully hidden so you won't be seen.
Someday we will return and find thee again,
May you live in safety and in happiness till then."

The farewells took several minutes as the visitors did not really want to leave and the hosts could not bear the thought of their leaving. Shamir stroked Absom then Cita. Cheeku stood on Absom's shoulder and groomed him, much as monkeys groom each other. Meela also hugged and kissed both Lena and the human friends who had meant so much to her beloved Cheeku.

Shamir joined trunks with Lena and the two stood there for a long time, dreading letting go of one another. Shamir promised to mark the trees with the juice of berries as the herd moved on making it easier to find them.

At last Absom sighed, "We have to go Lena."

Lena sat down so that Absom and Cita could prepare for the journey. She waited patiently while they loaded their camping gear, then climbed aboard. Lena looked back longingly at Shamir, then turned her face toward home.

"Good-bye White One. Good-bye little Monkeys. We promise to come again." In a few minutes, they had disappeared into the rain forest.

Cheeku, Meela and Shamir stood silently for a long time, then walked back to join the herd and tell them the news from Toungoo.

Little Borga was happy to hear that her mother was well, and Maru was also pleased. They wept at the death of Emma, but rejoiced that most members of the family now in captivity were well.

That night Shamir slept fitfully. He was so relieved that Absom was safe and was in charge of the elephants in Burma. However, now that he had found Lena, there was a heartfelt emptiness without her beside him.

Cheeku, sensing the unhappiness of his friend reminded him, "They promised to return."

"I know," Shamir sighed, "I shall look forward to that time when we are together again, and until then, treasure the memories of these golden days."

Cheeku patted his friend gently, "I know Shamir. The value of true friendship can never be expressed in words. In my heart, I know that you and Lena will be together again, someday. Absom will see to it."

"You are a great comfort, Cheeku. We will find helpful and productive ways to fill our days until they come again."

And with that, they slept, contentedly, with memories of past good times and dreams of future adventures filling their heads.

The two friends moved to the place where Absom and his young bride slept. Shamir wept with joy as he saw that his young friend, now a grown man, lay sleeping peacefully, embraced by a beautiful young woman.

Epilogue

A little less than two years after Absom, Cita and Lena returned from the rain forest and their visit with Shamir, a most wondrous event occurred. A beautiful white baby elephant was born to Lena. This elephant caused quite a stir in the kingdom because at no other time had a white elephant been born in captivity.

King Burengnong rejoiced as did his son Prince Risha.

Lena was the happiest of all about the birth of the white calf. Forever he would remind her of her beloved Shamir. While the rest of the kingdom called the elephant, "Little White One," she called him Shama, after both his mother and father.

Several months before Shama was born, Cita had given birth to a baby girl. She and Absom were thrilled with the birth of their first child who they named, Lahni.

It was three years after the birth of Shama before Absom took his family to visit the rain forest again. While Lena carried Absom, Cita, and the child, Lahni, on their return trip to the rain forest the baby white elephant was not with them. Little White One was not allowed out of the palace grounds. In fact, the king had built a special stable for him right next door to the palace. Only the king's most trusted guards cared for Little White One. Absom had waited to take the trip until Lena had completed nursing the calf, and his own little girl was old enough to travel with them.

Shamir and Lena had agreed upon a special way he would mark the trees to show her the way to his present home. Absom sensed that Lena knew where she was going and allowed her to lead the way. They found Shamir with greater ease than one might have thought possible after five long years.

Shamir was resting after his afternoon meal when he saw his friends approach. Needless to say, he was delighted to see them again.

Lena shared with Shamir all the events that had occurred in the past five years, and Absom introduced his daughter to Shamir.

"Isn't Lahni beautiful, Shamir? Don't you think she looks like her mother?" Absom bragged.

The little girl did look much like beautiful Cita.

Shamir had a new friend to show them also. Cheeku and Meela had both died during the past year. He missed them terribly but they had lived almost twenty years, long and full lives for monkeys. They had left in Shamir's care a little grandson who had been orphaned. They had left him with Shamir because he was an albino monkey and needed special care and attention in order to survive in the forest. Shamir called the monkey, Cheela.

Absom and Cita admired the monkey, but little Lahni was overjoyed with him. She played with him almost constantly.

Before the party returned home to Burma, it was decided that Cheela would be a wonderful playmate for Lahni and for Shama, the baby elephant, as well. Shamir knew that the little monkey would be well cared for and probably had a

117

greater chance to survive with Absom. However, Absom promised Shamir that he would bring the monkey with them on their next visit.

"I promise we will not wait so long next time, Shamir."

The good-byes were again long and full of tears and much hugging and stroking, but each carried the hope that another visit would happen in the near future.

Indeed, many visits did occur.

THE END

GLOSSARY

This Glossary contains the names of most of the characters in the story and foreign and/or unusual words used in the story.

Absom - Servant to Lyling, the elephant catcher who becomes trainer of Shamir

Akbar - Ruler of India in the 16th Century

Bengal, Bay of - Bay which extends from the eastern shores of India, along the western shores of Burma and is the destination of the Mouths of the Ganges River

Borga - Daughter of Hannah, sister of Maru

Borga (Little) - Daughter of Borga

Burengnong - Ruler of Burma during the 16th Centry

Burma - Country east of India in southeast Asia

Cheeku - A white monkey who becomes Shamir's close friend

Chin Hills - A high hilly region in western Burma

Chittagong - City in India located on the Bay of Bengal in what is now Bangledesh

Cita - Daughter of the fisherman, Moglee and Jahlona

Emma - Sister of Hannah

Ganges River - Principal river in India which flows From the high Himalayas in north central India to the eastern border of what is now Bengladesh but was part of India at the time of the story.

Hannah - Queen of the herd and Shamir's grandmother

Hasti - Indian word meaning elephant

India - Large country in South Asia on the Indian subcontinent

119

Irrawaddy River - Principal river in Burma

Jahlona - Wife of Moglee and mother of Cita

Jaku - Son of Emma

Kasha - Elephant catcher for Akbar, Mogul ruler of India

Khedda - Rounding up of an entire herd of elephants through the use of a wall of fire, a corral and several trained elephants

Koonkies - Trained elephants

Kreeto - Guard of the royal elephants in Burma

Lena - Absom's elephant, Sheba's daughter and a friend to Shamir

Lyling - Elephant catcher for Burengnong, ruler of Burma

Machi - Assistant elephant catcher to Kasha

Mahout - An elephant trainer

Martaban, Gulf of - Body of water at the southeastern part of Burma

Maru - Mother of Shamir and daughter of Hannah

Meela - A monkey, friend of Cheeku

Moglee - a fisherman from Chittagong

Pagan - The ancient capital of Burma

Prome - A city in Burma

Ramsa - A monkey, uncle of Meela

Risha - Prince of Burma who is a good friend of Absom.

Shamir - The white elephant, son of Maru and Simbu

Sheba - Lyling's elephant and mother of Lena

Simbu - Shamir's father

Sittang River - River in Burma, site of Toungoo

Toungoo - Capital of Burma in the 16th Century

Also mentioned in the story are: **Cali, Jano, Janu** (Other children of Maru); **Lannie, Kisha, Talman, Delpha, Kaltus** (Other members of the herd**); Kordo**, an older white elephant, at the court of Burengnong

Beverly Croskery is a former teacher, principal, and Curriculum Director. She has also been a television teacher (ROMPER ROOM) and script writer for both public and commercial television. Since retiring from Northwest Local Schools in Cincinnati, she has enjoyed consulting and completing her first children's book. Beverly enjoys reading, tennis, and storytelling. She and husband, Robert, a retired clergyman, love to travel and visit their six grandchildren.

Bonny Bregante is a free lance artist who lives in Georgia with her husband, Mark, and son, Christian. Her favorite subjects to draw and paint are children and animals. Bonny is also an accomplished sculptor.

Richard Croskery, who drew our map, is a physician in Greenville, North Carolina, where he lives with his wife, Andrea and children, Robin and Thomas. When a busy medical practice allows, he enjoys drawing and playing the clarinet. Richard is the son of the author.

How To Order Your Own Autographed Copies of *SHAMIR, THE WHITE ELEPHANT*

Call **513-542-9819** with your VISA or Master Card order or send this order form to **Bell-Forsythe Publishers; 5300 Hamilton Ave., Ste. 1000; Cincinnati, OH 45224**

_____ copies of *SHAMIR,* at $14.95 each $_____
        ($13.95 each when ordering 4 or more copies.)

+ $2.50 Book Rate shipping for first book, $_____
$1.00 for each additional book.

                   TOTAL $_____

Please allow three weeks for delivery

MAIL TO: (Please print clearly and include phone number)

_____

_____

_____

_____

FREE AUTOGRAPH

If you would like your copies autographed, please print the name or names to be inscribed.

_____

_____

Payment Made by: ___check ___Master Card ___VISA

Card No._____Expires Mo____ Yr____

Signature_____